I0621985

All Mine

A 1Night Stand Collection

By
Kerry Adrienne

This book is a work of fiction. Names, characters, places, and incidents are the products of the author's imagination or used fictitiously. Any resemblance to actual events, locales or persons, living or dead, is entirely coincidental.

Copyright © 2016 by Kerry Adrienne
ISBN: 978-1-68361-080-9
Cover art by Mina Carter

All rights reserved. Except for use in any review, the reproduction or utilization of this work, in whole or in part, in any form by any electronic, mechanical or other means now known or hereafter invented, is forbidden without the written permission of the publisher.

Published by Decadent Publishing Company, LLC
Look for us online at:
www.decadentpublishing.com

Senator, Mine

Book 1

Dedication

To my Prince....

Senator, Mine

Eleanor's romantic tour of Italy shatters when her long-time boyfriend dumps her in Pompeii. Hoping an evening with a handsome Roman might save her trip, she contacts Madame Eve at 1Night Stand, then goes out to explore, buying a small golden signet in a mysterious antiquities shop near the Forum.

Darius, a hard-working Senator in Ancient Rome, is puzzled by the Sibyl's words: You will not find love in your lifetime. Following her directions, he spots Eleanor, a barbarian wearing his stolen senator's ring.

A night spent together may be just what they both need to break down the columns of time that stand between them.

Chapter One

Eleanor made up her mind the instant she saw the sign, hand-scrawled in English. *Antiquities Shop.* She would buy something to help her forget about Peter.

She pushed the wooden door open and stepped inside. She'd been dumped before, but to be jilted while touring Pompeii—unforgivable. Peter had known how much she'd looked forward to visiting the archaeological site, and it had been cruel of him to break off the relationship as soon as the tour bus doors opened. He'd left her standing at one of the gated entrances to the ruined city and walked off toward New Pompeii without a backward glance. After that, the only ashes she could think of were the remains of four years of her life.

She had continued the tour alone. Rieti, Terracina, and Tivoli had blurred under her grief. As she entered Rome, her heartache had turned to frustration, with both Peter and herself. The Eternal City beckoned to her with its alluring charm, promising absolution. Or at least great shopping.

She opened her eyes wide in an attempt to see better in the darkened room. Rome would be hers. In spite of Peter. She took another step inside and the door clattered shut behind her, blocking the sunlight.

She shivered at the sudden change in temperature. July in Rome sweltered, and few places she'd visited offered air conditioning. The shop provided a welcome respite, though the coolness felt like a dusty museum's chill, all marble and effigies.

"Hello?" As her vision adjusted to the dim light, the wares became more visible. Rows of shelves brimming with treasure and junk alike lined the walls. Grotesque statuary stood in fierce opposition to finer-chiseled figures, and pottery spilled in piles from every vacant spot. A narrow walkway led through the jumble of antiques and artifacts.

She clutched her shoulder strap and stepped into the fray of relics. Good thing Peter, the shopping downer, wasn't here.

The scent of age hung in the shop. Dust and dirt—once a king's ransom—and tithes to long-forgotten gods circulated in the cool air. The familiar warm odor of decaying papyri comforted her. Peter had always teased her about her archaeologist's nose. Not anymore. She wondered if he'd planned to return to Indiana at all, or if the whole trip had been a ruse to get her to fund his travels and escape from the United States. She had expected him to propose. Imagine that!

"Hello?" Why was she obsessing about Peter instead of enjoying her trip? "Is anyone here?" She ran her fingers over the surface of a deep silver bowl set at chest height on the first row of shelving, touching the dents and ridges the bowl had suffered from hard use.

"Yes," a soft voice laden with a thick Italian accent filtered through the clutter. "Do you need help? Ah, it's you. Madame Eve emailed you would be coming."

She pushed the bowl back onto the shelf. Had Madame Eve already found a match? A good-looking Italian guy with no baggage? *Wait! How does he know about Madame Eve*? "I'd like to find a memento," she called out, louder than she had intended. She wiped damp shaking palms across her shirt. "Something to remind me of Rome." Shopping therapy to ease the pain.

"What did you have in mind?" A man stepped from behind a shelf of old texts right in front of her.

She took a step backward and wobbled, off-balance at his sudden appearance. Was he the one Madame Eve had chosen?

He smiled broadly, his white teeth almost glowing against his tan face. "No, I am not. Your date is considerably...younger."

Eleanor blinked, startled. "Uh, okay. I don't know. I'd like something small." She fidgeted. "It's difficult to explain but I'll know it when I see it, I guess." Her head spun. Maybe the 1Night Stand idea hadn't been a good one. She'd been in the hotel room researching things to do in Rome when she'd found the website. Her anger toward Peter had given her the confidence to fill out the form and request a match. But a random storekeeper shouldn't know all that...or answer questions she hadn't asked aloud.

The man's wrinkled face concealed his dark eyes as he scowled in thought. His clothing was garish and colorful, overstated. Was he a gypsy? She had been warned about scams and sales tactics aimed at tourists. Maybe shopping here wasn't such a good idea, either. She backed away. Things were too weird.

"Don't worry," he said. "You don't need to fear me. Which time period did you have in mind? Hadrian? Constantine? Republic?" He rubbed his hands together.

Her mouth opened. "Ovid," she blurted. "Do you have anything from Ovid's time? Something affordable?"

She and Peter had loved to read Ovid's bawdy love poetry aloud, either in English or Latin depending on how many beers they had drunk. The more, the better.

"Ovid," the shopkeeper muttered. "Ovid.

Augustus... Hmmm. 10 BC or so." He shook his head and then closed his eyes. "Yes, that is an excellent time period."

She waited, listening to the droning of the one fluorescent light. Well, he wasn't too pushy. She grinned. The thought of meeting her date later certainly had spiced the day up. She'd need to head back to the hotel soon to shower and dress. And meet the hot Italian.

"I have just the thing." The old man's dark eyes snapped open, lit with the glow of accomplishment. "Yes, a fine time in Roman history. You like jewelry, don't you?" he asked, walking off toward the far end of the aisle. "Of course you do. Follow me."

Eleanor slung her pack over her shoulder and followed. Jewelry. Not likely. Too expensive. Too flashy.

As she walked, she gazed at the vast array of objects the man had accumulated. A baroque mirror propped against the side wall and she stopped to admire it, wincing at her reflection. *I look like something the cat dragged in.* She turned away.

"A little of everything here," the shopkeeper said.

She hadn't noticed he'd stopped and watched her. She ducked her head in embarrassment, and pushed her hair behind her ears.

"But the mirror is not from Ovid's time. You won't need that." He laughed and motioned for her to follow.

At the back of the shop, he slipped behind a glass counter covered with trinkets. She stood on the other side of the display, waiting to see what he would suggest.

He bent and jingled a set of keys. The lock squeaked and the glass door vibrated in its track as he pulled it aside. How many tourists came in the little shop, or even noticed the sign? No one else was in the store although it sat right across from the Forum. *How odd.*

"Here. The perfect memento for you. Madame Eve would approve for your date."

"And how do you know of Madame Eve?"

"Ah, just call me a facilitator. And don't worry, your secret is safe. I have kept many over the years. Don't you want to see this treasure?"

She scowled. The website had not mentioned any type of facilitator, yet the man knew about the match. Her stomach quivered at what the night might hold. Who cared if a lone shopkeeper knew? Not like she'd be returning here.

"Well?"

"What is it?" She moved closer to examine the object he held.

"A senator's ring from the time of Augustus." He waved the item with a flourish. "A rare and beautiful find, for a deserving young woman."

The golden circle sparkled in the half-light like the wedding band that shone in her dreams. She tried to control her sharp intake of breath.

"A rather personal memento, wouldn't you say?"

"It's beautiful."

"Indeed."

"Which senator?" Gorgeous. What a find. Was it legal to take it out of the country? Surely it held historical significance.

"Yes, it can be exported," the shopkeeper said. "We don't know who owned the signet, as many records of the Senate at that time were lost, but it has been cleared by the Antiquities Commission."

She hadn't mentioned exporting it aloud. Had he read her mind? No, that wasn't possible. She squirmed. Nothing about the shop or its contents felt normal. One thing was certain. The ring was amazing. And perfect.

"What does the engraving say?" she asked.

"Darius."

She drew in a quick breath, as a gasp of warm air breezed across her neck, making the hairs stand. She shuddered. *I've been watching too many old movies.*

"As common as the name was at the time, no senators named Darius are on any rolls." The shopkeeper pushed it closer to her face. "And Madame Eve recommends it. What do you say?"

"How much?" Eleanor whispered.

"Ah." The shopkeeper grinned. "What price would you pay for a little ring that will change your life forever?"

Chapter Two

Darius paced. He hadn't been to see the Sibyl in months, but her last words haunted him. *You will not find love in your lifetime.* He kicked the dirt with his shoe and a cloud of dust rose, swirling around his toga. The purple-striped senator's clothing annoyed him when in Rome, but wearing it on his journey to Tibur had been almost unbearable. With things heavy on his mind of late, he wanted the silence of the countryside to envelop him.

As was often the case, his status prevented the peace he sought. Politics in the Empire shifted under Augustus, and conflicts on many fronts caused heated debate in the Senate. Power, glory, recognition—he now found all of them tiresome. Wars in the Rhine had depleted his energy until he would almost exchange his senatorial toga for the simple tunic of the worker. Rome must be strong, but need it rule the entire world?

A line of men milled around the outside of the temple, awaiting audience with the seer. The Sibyl at Tibur was well renowned for her gift of sight and in her time at the temple, she had foreseen wars, plagues, and even lovers' trysts. The line to see her and gain a prophesy formed early and grew long.

Accepting the preference he got as a senator, he moved near the front of the line. He cursed under his breath. He was no better than the common whore, using his status for gratification of impulses. And yet, waiting all day in the hot sun was not something he was willing to withstand. The journey had already taken too long, and he wanted to return to his friend's villa by evening. A feast and bed awaited him, and the pick of any servant girl if he so chose. He shaded his eyes and looked out over the vibrant landscape. Tibur's magnificence was both natural and man-made, and many senators traveled here to relax and take a break from the hectic pace of Rome. Even Augustus visited the local waterfalls and temples.

The verdant hills grew tall around him, dotted with the white villas of the wealthy. His own home in Rome was impressive, but not as lavish as these buildings. Columns rose into travertine arches carved into intricate patterns, and the sun sparked off the facades, luring men to lust after the grandeur the town held.

In the deep gorge below, the Aniene River poured through a narrow channel. The massive cascades that spilled over the rocks at the gorge's entrance and down to the valley floor had excited him as a youngster. Today, he had no time for sight-seeing. He turned to survey the wait.

A few patricians stood ahead of him in line, and the midday sun scorched his back. He sighed. If only he could take off the toga and wear just the light tunic underneath. The ornate garment symbolized all that fouled his life. Too much pomp; too much work. Not enough time to enjoy the beauty of the world when every hour was spent trying to constrain things with the rule of law.

A magnificent brown hawk flew at the valley lip past the columned Temple of Vesta, and he watched it soar. The freedom of flight would serve him well. If he shed the bounds of man and lived more simply, perhaps he would find his happiness. But how could he leave behind the senate seat his father had worked so hard to secure? The regal bird alighted on the

Sibyl's temple, and screeched a long, piercing squall, cutting into Darius's heart like the shriek of the Sibyl. *Alone. Not free.*

The Sibyl's last words. At first, he'd dismissed them in the day-to-day trials and law discussions of the Senate. With wars and new laws, he had not had time to consider the implications her words held. He'd never completely believed the ranting of the woman, yet she drew him to her time and again with her promises and visions. Many men did place great weight on her prophecies, and her lure was unmistakable. The bird fluttered its great wings then sailed off to circle the temples again.

He remembered how, as a boy, he had stood staring out over this valley while his father had audience with the Sibyl. Now both his parents gone to the beyond, their funeral pyres still burning in his soul. How did life pass so quickly? He'd lived twenty-eight years and had yet to find a wife. With another shriek, the hawk dove into the canyon and Darius rushed to the low wall to watch it until it was a mere speck among the green. To follow it would mean happiness.

"Water, sir?"

He turned. A slave girl, dark hair pulled high on her head, held a wooden bowl out to him. He nodded, and she raised it to his lips. He drank, the coolness splashing down his throat like the waterfall into the gorge. Sweet refreshment.

The girl moved on to the next man in line, her willowy form swaying as she carried the heavy vessel. She couldn't have been more than sixteen, and she wouldn't get the option to marry, except by force. He grimaced. That was not marriage. He wanted a woman to choose him. It didn't make him less of a man. Why did he worry about finding a wife when senatorial things kept him busy for days on end? His duty was to serve Emperor Augustus, not fulfill his own life. His head throbbed and he shielded his eyes from the sun. There had to be more.

One man stood ahead of him now, waiting to hear words that may or may not please him. Men came to the Sibyl seeking love, wealth, gambling secrets. Did any ask for happiness? He turned to find the slave girl. She had made her way down the line a good way, and she carried the water without complaint. Was she happy? He shook his head. He should be happy that he was not a slave, rather than lamenting being a senator.

Guards stood on either side of the temple entrance and waved men in at the appropriate time. No one exited at this doorway. After an audience with the Sibyl, one left via an arched opening on the other side of the temple. The whole event orchestrated for efficiency.

A bell chimed. Time for another person to enter. The guards motioned. The patrician was old, bent, and crept to the entrance. Did he wish for his youth? Longer life? Did he harbor regrets?

He stepped into the temple's shadow, where the coolness of shade and marble settled over him. Musky incense drifted out through the doorway and mixed with the scent of summer flowers. Closing his eyes, he breathed in the sweetness then exhaled. It was good to get out of the city for a few days.

The sun headed toward the hilltops and the shadows grew longer in the glade of olive trees surrounding the temple complex. She did not see people after sunset and many of those waiting would have to stay in line overnight then lose their position to anyone of a higher social order who happened to show up in the morning. He sighed.

Ding! The guards motioned him to enter. His throat filled with the acid of anticipation.

He stopped inside the temple, waiting for his vision to adjust to the darkness. Oil lamps flickered in alcoves down the narrow hallway, their smoke casting a hazy glaze through the air and mixing with musky tendrils of wafting incense. The guards would not lead him; he knew where to go. He followed the corridor for about twenty paces, running his hand along the cool marble walls as he walked. So many men had gone before him, seeking answers. Many would follow. He stepped into the circular open area at the end of the hallway and stood, waiting. Statues mounted on tall pillars lined the walls. The staircase to the Sibyl lay in the center of the room, leading down into darkness. His stomach trembled. What would she say to him? Why did he care? He should have stayed in Rome and sated his lust in the brothel.

He recognized most of the chiseled gods and demigods towering above him, but a statue of an unfamiliar child caught his attention. The carved girl held an amphora, smiling. He imagined her, rosy cheeked and warm, walking along the rocky road, carrying oil home for her family. A family he would never have. Though the emperor encouraged, indeed rewarded, marriage and children, there had been little time or desire to find the right partner. And what woman would want a husband who might be sent to a remote outpost or to war at any time? He wanted a companion in all things. Not just a slave or lover.

A low gong sounded and vibrated through his chest. Taking a deep breath, he moved to the center of the chamber. He pulled out his money pouch and tossed a few coins into the altar bowl. Time.

He made his way to the bottom of the rock staircase waiting again for his vision to adapt to the stygian darkness. The incense whorled heavier there, mixed with the sulfurous fumes permeating the chamber. He coughed. The walls were slippery rock, leaden with humidity from the springs below. A cave for the old woman.

For a brief moment, the air cleared, and a form reclining on a stone bench at the far side of the room sat up. The Sibyl.

"Darius," she rasped. "You return."

"I do." He stepped closer.

A lone oil lamp sat to one side of the bench, and its smoke wavered around the seer like a mass of snakes. Not wanting to appear disrespectful, he stifled another cough.

She leaned forward.

"I had a vision. Eve appeared to me. She said you would return, seeking happiness."

Asking questions while the Sibyl canted was pointless. She saw, she spoke. He waited.

"You wish for love, but you have to learn to let go of unimportant things. You think you know what you want, but you have not experienced all. Time will guide you."

He bowed his head. She always spoke in riddles. Deciphering the senators was difficult enough. This was mad.

"You do not believe." The Sibyl rose. "Until you let go of all, you cannot experience all."

"What would you have me do?" He put his hands on his hips and frowned. Her eyes widened and she stepped toward him. Incense trails followed her as she walked and the light from the oil lamp backlit her form.

"Eve suggests a rendezvous. After a night, return to me with what you have learned."

"Who is Eve?" He squinted, eyes watering from the heavy smoke. "Rendezvous with whom? Where?"

"Patience." She mumbled under her breath, chanting and waving her arms slowly as she made her way back to the bench and sat. She closed her eyes, and the muttering continued.

Was she finished? Darius listened for the gong to signal his time had ended, but no sound swept through the cave other than the low chant. He stepped closer, but the words she had spoken held no meaning. If he wanted a rendezvous, he'd return to his friend's villa for the evening. Or find a whorehouse. Tibur was overrun with women for sale.

Her eyes flew open and he backed away. She looked beyond him. "Your test waits in the olive grove. Take her unto the riverbank where the hawk's call ended, near a small cascade. Beside it is a cavern. There, you will both find what you seek."

He waited. The Sibyl often sent men on quests, but he had never been given one. What did it mean? "Who is Eve?" he repeated.

"She has offered to help you. Meet with the girl in the grove. Return to me tomorrow."

He rubbed his arms. Maybe he did need a night with someone. Perhaps he could gain perspective.

"Do you agree to the challenge?"

"Uh, yes. I think the idea is sound." He had no choice. It would be foolish to refuse her. He'd suspend his worry for an evening, and the physical closeness might free his mind.

"Return to me on day's light tomorrow." The Sibyl closed her eyes again and folded her hands.

"But...."

A low gong sounded, echoed through the room, and vibrated in his belly. He rubbed his face and made his way to the staircase.

Chapter Three

Eleanor adjusted her pack on her shoulders and stood at the curb, waiting to cross the *Via dei Fori Imperiali*. The crumbled ruins of the Roman Forum spread out on the opposite side of the road like shell fragments scattered along the shore after a violent storm. She clutched her newly acquired treasure and joined the horde of tourists sweeping across the road in a giant swarming wave as drivers tried to skim past without hitting anyone. People, pointing and posing alongside the entrance to the ruins, clamored and chatted.

For a moment, she wished she had stayed longer in the little shop. At least it was quiet. And much cooler. She closed her eyes and squeezed the ring, taking comfort in its smoothness. *Darius.* She'd have to research the senator when she got back to the hotel. For now, she had to figure out if she could go through with her hasty 1Night Stand commitment. A night to remember forever was the promise, but was it the right thing to do? She hadn't expected a match to happen so quickly.

She turned to face the past and stepped onto the stone walkway that meandered through the ruins. The Forum sprawled before her. Rome, its glory crumbled around her like old dreams, beckoned her closer. Her relationship with Peter hadn't lasted long enough to make its mark on the world. Not a pebble remained of their shared glory. Had it been a mirage? Or a mistake? To invest so much in something so new felt out of place here in the Eternal City.

Yet the powerful Rome had fallen, too, and left its secrets scattered along the *Via Sacra*. If such a nation couldn't stand the test of time, how could she expect love to last past a fleeting moment? What right had she to demand more?

Her time in Rome had become a therapy session.

A laughing couple jostled her as they passed, oblivious. The woman twirled a single red rose. The 1Night Stand encounter was just what she needed. No one would ever have to know.

She strolled through the grassy Forum, holding the signet ring close to her chest, trying to reconstruct the temples and buildings she had studied. The *Curia* rose high above her on the right, its brown stucco shedding and peeling. She imagined senators' discourse rising from the crowd in the *Comitium*, the courtyard in front of the *Curia*. Beside the *Curia* stood the *Plutei of Trajan* with its chiseled façade of marble. The detailed relief in the arch's carvings astonished her, and she peered up for several minutes, trying to decipher the Latin engravings.

People moved sluggishly and with less enthusiasm. Rome was so hot. The ring grew slick in her wet palms, but she hesitated to put it in her pack.

Temples and houses seemed to morph out of the Palatine Hill, watching the goings-on like gods looking down from the heavens.

Her head ached and the heavy air filled her lungs.

The backpack felt like it had grown in both size and weight and she slipped it off her shoulders and onto the ground. She pushed her hair aside and sat down on a large, squared stone under the Temple of Saturn to rest.

Tourists of every nationality swarmed the paths among the ruins, their chatter a dull droning, mixed with the clicking of digital shutters and narration for home video recorders. Despite the break-up, Rome lived up to her expectations. The city was magnificent. Tonight would be the cherry on top. Who wouldn't want to spend the night in the arms of a handsome Italian man?

A flock of pigeons swirled overhead, awaiting crumbs from sidewalk vendor's snacks. Did birds flock so brazenly over old Rome?

The ring had grown warm in her hand. Its smooth gold marred by the engraver's tool, which had left a perfectly formed name in the middle of one side where the characteristic flattened surface lay. *Darius*. The mysterious senator. Had he dined with Ovid?

"You okay, miss?"

She peered at the man standing over her. His thick English startled her out of her musings. A beggar?

"Please," he said, "have a rose." He grinned and held out a long-stemmed, pink blossom.

Gladiator or Praetorian Guardsman? Senator? His diminutive size put him out of place in her daydreams, and she tried to stifle a chuckle.

"Funny?" The man asked, his smile less genuine. His dark hair curled in every direction and he tried to hide the beginnings of a scowl. He pulled the flower back.

"Oh, no. Please forgive me. I meant no disrespect." She stood and brushed off her backside with a sweep of her hand. She picked up her pack.

"Rose? One US dollar. You are American?"

"Yes, I am American. No rose." Would Peter have bought her one? Not likely. It would have been a frivolous expense.

He stood, holding the flower out to her.

"I'm sorry," she said. "I am allergic."

"*Bene.*" The man walked off to approach the next tourist with his floral assault.

Men. An image of Peter, sweating and trying to sell roses on the Forum, lightened her mood. She giggled and clasped the signet. *If only.* The punishment would be just.

"I wonder if your owner was such a little man," she said to the ring. It slipped and fell to the ground, taking a single bounce where she had been sitting. She scooped it up, noticing a portion of an inscription on the rock. *Tempo incognoscio.*

"Time cannot be known?" she translated in a whisper, leaning down and fingering the carved lettering. "Or, time is not to be known? Or is not understood?"

A hawk spiraled over the Forum, shrieking. Its slow circular descent shadowed across her. Startled, she jumped up, and her head spun from the rapid change of position. *Whoa....*

She slipped the signet onto her index finger so she wouldn't drop it again. Her legs weakened as the dizziness overtook her and the world blackened.

Chapter Four

A *m I dead*? A bird called overhead and Eleanor opened her eyes. Where were the buildings? She sat up. Moss? There wasn't any moss in the Forum. And all this vegetation. *Crap*! She felt around for her pack. Gone. *What the hell*? She searched behind her. Not there. She stood, steadying herself against a trunk. An olive grove. She must still be in Italy. The lightheadedness threatened to return and she held her head. After a moment she moved her hands from her face and, still leaning for support, twisted the ring on her finger. Trees with silvery leaves and cascading white flowers lined long rows in front of her as far as she could see. The Forum was gone.

Don't panic. Count to ten.

"Eve said I would find you here."

Eleanor turned to see a tall man standing about twenty feet away. His dark hair cropped short and his broad shoulders wrapped in a...*toga*? She blinked. "Madame Eve didn't tell me how this works," she said, walking toward the Roman god. Damn, he was handsome. She gulped. "Do you know?"

He shook his head. His warm skin tone set off his deep brown eyes and his chiseled features would have inspired sculptors.

"The Sibyl said Eve wanted me to find you here and take you down to the river." He adjusted his money pouch on his hip and she trailed her gaze down to gaze at the complicated folds that she hoped concealed a bottom half as honed as his upper body.

"Hello?" She held out her hand. "I'm Eleanor. Nice to meet you."

He looked down at her gesture then back to her face. At least they'd sent a hunk. Maybe he wasn't very smart, but he didn't have to be, did he?

He reached out and took her hand and she shivered from the strength and warmth of his grasp. Her heart thudded. She would have no problems going through with this night.

"I am Darius." He tugged. "Follow me." Her head spun—again. Darius, the owner of the ring, was her 1Night Stand. Passing out a second time in a day would be humiliating. He was more man than she could have hoped for, and the authentic-looking wardrobe completed the picture.

"What's down at the river?" She didn't see any hotels in the olive grove.

He pressed his lips to her fingers and then his grip tightened. "How did you come by my ring?" he growled. "I lost it in a northern battle."

His gaze tore into her for a moment and the rushing water's echo through the trees grew louder in the quiet. She could play along. Madame Eve was good. "I bought it from a merchant near the Forum."

"It was not his to sell, but as I have been told to take care of you tonight, you may wear it. Tomorrow, you will return it to me."

This guy played his part well. "Okay, I'll give it back to you in the morning."

He glared at her as if he was questioning her trustworthiness, then he smiled.

"Now, where are we going?"

"Come." He pulled her along behind him. "I'll show you."

She allowed it. What else could she to do? She'd signed up for the 1Night Stand and the thought of being with this man warmed her heart and then some.

Darius growled. Her pale skin and blonde hair marked her as a barbarian from the north. He led her through the grove toward the river, holding her small hand in his. The Sibyl must have great plans for him to send him to bed a barbarian. The mysterious Eve must be influential, indeed. He sneaked a glance at Eleanor. Her long, flowing hair should be tied up in plaits and curls, not falling around her shoulders like a horse's mane. The Sibyl was testing him. He would complete her instructions and relieve his body. Then the seer would reveal his path to love. And he would get his ring back—a bonus.

"How did you get to Tibur?" he asked as they walked. "A long journey from the north. Did you arrive by foot?"

"I, uh, woke up in the olive grove. I have no idea how I got here."

He scowled. She must have arrived with a shipment of slaves from the north, yet she didn't look like a slave. Her clothes, very minimal, were unfamiliar. Perhaps she served in a wealthy household. No matter.

"This way." He strode along, anxious to reach their destination

She stumbled. "Slow down." He caught her and for a moment, stared into her blue eyes. He'd fly in that azure sky and be free, even if only for a moment. He made sure she held her balance then let her go. She giggled. No, she didn't act like a slave at all.

"We have to hurry," he said. "The sun is almost gone." Even in the rosy glow of late day, he could see the paleness of her skin. His heart thumped. He'd not bedded many barbarians, and none as lovely as she. Perhaps the test would not be so difficult, after all. How it would lead to his fulfillment was a mystery, but he had faith that he followed the path the Sibyl said he should be on. He linked their fingers, and they walked on in silence.

At the water's edge, he dropped her hand and peered up at the edge of the rocky walls where the temples stood. The hawk had dived and headed to the greater falls farther up the canyon.

"This place is magical," she sighed.

He admired her profile, the short turned-up nose and small chin so different from the Roman women's strong features. A passing gust blew her hair about her face, and he reached to smooth the loose strands. She faced him. "Thank you."

He trembled, unused to being so gentle with a woman. She smiled. Oh, the gods had not prepared him to gaze upon her this way. He pressed his mouth against hers and a fire shot through his stomach and down his body. Her soft lips parted. He pushed the kiss firmly and then drew back, humbled to see her eyes flutter open, yet remained heavy-lidded. His cock ached and he adjusted his toga to conceal his throbbing erection.

"There *is* magic here."

"Indeed." She stared out over the river.

"We need to hurry before night overtakes us." He whispered, the moment near perfect in its silence and beauty.

"Okay," she said. "If we must."

"We'll have time to get to know each other when we reach our destination." He drew her close and she propped her arm against his chest.

"Promise?" she said, eyes twinkling.

"Oh, yes," he growled. "Let's get going."

He led her upstream along the narrow path. They would reach the falls within a short time at their pace.

He'd never met a barbarian with such beauty and

intelligence. She wasn't afraid of him and seemed to study the world around her with intensity. Perhaps she was a figment of his imagination. The kiss said otherwise.

Tree roots jumbled and crisscrossed the dirt in front of him. "Be careful. You might fall." He held her hand and stepped over the first knot of roots, his foot slipping on the dampness.

"I can do it." She laughed and slipped her hand away. "You first."

He lifted the edge of his toga and stepped onto the embankment and then glanced back to watch Eleanor navigate the maze with ease. He scowled. Her odd shoes, laced with strange ties, and her short clothing allowed her more grace of movement than he had.

"Why are you wearing only undergarments?"

She laughed. "These aren't undergarments, silly. Shorts and a T-shirt."

He frowned. The Sibyl had given him an odd task. "Are you a slave, then?"

"No. Of course not." She beamed at him and he ducked his head. Confusion tore through him.

"Then you must be a barbarian." Everything about the way she dressed screamed it. But her manner did not fit.

She shook her head.

They strolled in silence alongside the coursing river. A few flying star insects blinked in the early evening's duskiness. He longed to shed his toga and feel the air on his skin, but it wasn't time for that. They had to make it to the cave.

A thin waterfall splashed into a clear pool. Trees branches left tracing lines in the water. A swim would cool the day's heat. Perhaps she would join him. Lust surged in his groin.

"I don't think I have ever seen such a beautiful

place."

He'd not been this far into the canyon before. The land held many secrets.

"It is beautiful and mysterious. I will check for the cave where we are to spend the night."

Surprise passed over her face, but she nodded. "Okay. I'm going to sit for a moment."

He watched her drink in the scene. The kiss lingered on his lips. So sweet. The one-night rendezvous would be welcome. Perhaps the Sibyl did know what he needed.

He lingered, not wanting to leave her. But he had to find the cave before it got any darker or they'd be spending the night on the riverbank.

A faint glimmer of an oil lamp sparked near the edge of the falls. The entrance.

The cavern was high enough to stand in, but Eleanor crouched, shivering in the damp room. The evening grew cool and she wished she had a jacket. The closed-in space confined her, but the oil lamps helped dispel the darkness except around the edges. Hopefully, there weren't any creepy crawlies—the stone floor appeared swept clean. Earthen smells mixed with musky incense.

"This is where we stay tonight." Darius pointed to a straw-filled mattress in the corner, stacks of white woolen blankets piled high around it. On a low table, a bit of glowing ash in a seashell sat beside a small box.

"It's...nice." She moved to the table. Incense. She picked up the rainbow-hued shell and held it close to her nose.

"Abalone," he said. "That shell traveled from the sea."

She inhaled the aroma and relaxation swept through her. Madame Eve had provided a gorgeous setting. She set the shell down, picked up the rectangular wooden container, and lifted the lid to find several packets of condoms.

Her face flushed. This Roman god was hers for the night. If she had any doubts about the rendezvous, it was too late now.

"What is in the box?"

"Uh." She grabbed a packet then fumbled to put the lid back on. "Supplies."

"We are well provisioned." He pointed to a woven basket and two decanters near the cave wall. "Looks like we have food and wine."

"I'm starving." Thankfully he didn't ask for more details. Perhaps he had other things on his mind. She stuffed the plastic pack into her shorts pocket.

He smiled at her and touched her face. "Let's eat by the water. We can talk."

She sighed. Why couldn't she find a caring man like Darius on her own?

He picked up the basket and a decanter and headed to the cave entrance, his toga trailing on the floor. "Bring a blanket and one of the oil lamps."

Her stomach growled. She hadn't eaten since breakfast—probably why she had fainted. She pushed the ring higher on her finger then grabbed a blanket and one of the lamps and followed him out into the evening. The last of the sunset streaked the western edge of the sky. *Gorgeous.*

"Over here."

She turned to see him unwrapping his toga. Surely they would eat first? She gulped. The shadows made his muscles stand out in stark contrast. Mischief sparkled in his dark eyes.

"I don't like to eat with this heavy garment on."

The lamp teetered in her hand. She stumbled toward him, her gaze never wavering from the striking sight. His long woolen wrap fell away and her breath caught in her throat.

He wore a tunic underneath. Thank goodness. His thick legs bulged with muscle and his strong arms flexed as he draped the toga over a bush. The belted tunic was light, but not white like the toga, and it accented his olive skin and dark hair. She hoped he didn't mind her stares.

"Give me the blanket. I'll spread it out." He smiled. "Set the lamp on the ground over there." He pointed.

She obeyed. All part of the ruse, right? A strong gladiator was every woman's fantasy. Well, Darius wasn't a gladiator, but he sure looked like the ones she'd seen in movies. The familiar pang of desire grew in the pit of her stomach like a creeping vine. The night was going to be one to remember. If she could get through it without making a fool of herself drooling over him.

He flipped the blanket open and it ruffled to the ground. She stood to the side, watching him bend to slip off his shoes. He set them down and retrieved the basket of food.

"Join me." He sat down and crossed his legs. When she didn't move, he patted the ground.

She hesitated. Was he like a Scotsman—with nothing under his kilt? For just meeting the man a few hours ago, her imagination ran wild. Something about him took her over the edge.

"Here," he said, pointing to the blanket. "Let's eat. I thought you were hungry."

"I am." If only he knew how much.

She settled next to him, and the heat from his body invaded the air around her. He smelled of forest and leather and linen. The vine of desire grew and tightened. She'd never been with a man so—manly.

"How do you come to be here?" He took a long, thin roll out of the basket and she drank in the smell of the browned wheat. Her empty stomach clenched, and her mouth watered.

"I came from the United States," she said. "To visit."

He ripped off a piece of and held it out to her. "I've not heard of that place. It must be in the north."

She stuffed the bread in her mouth without regard to decorum and mumbled, "West."

A few stars glittered in the now-dark sky. The yellow glow from the oil lamp shadowed half of his chiseled face, accenting his strong Roman features. She yearned for closeness so she scooted nearer to him, her body touching his, but just barely.

"You don't act like a barbarian." He picked off small pieces and put them in his mouth, chewing slowly.

"I've told you. I'm not a barbarian."

"But you are light-skinned and fair-haired." He paused and watched her. For a moment, she imagined he really could be a senator in Rome, his strength guiding men and leading armies.

"Madame Eve didn't tell me this meeting would mimic ancient times. I don't know how to answer you."

He tore off another hunk of bread and his gaze traveled to the pool of water where the falls splashed. She untied her shoes and set them beside the blanket. The cooler air breezed over her bare feet and she closed her eyes. She couldn't remember the last time she had been so relaxed.

"What do you know of this Eve? The Sibyl mentioned her, and now you have said her name several times."

She stretched out and leaned back on her arms. Desire pooled. He was hers for the night. And Madame Eve had arranged it.

"I only know what I read online. She matched us

for the night, hoping it will solve our individual problems, or at least give us respite."

"You can read?" He flipped the basket lid open and dug in the contents. "And what do you mean, online? You speak in riddles, like the Sibyl."

"Of course I can read." A lone bird called in the night. "And online, on a computer." Surely this role playing would get old soon. Did he perform in local theater? He was a master at staying in character. More likely he was a model for some Italian couture line or maybe romance novel covers.

"A reading barbarian. I would never have suspected." He took out a bunch of deep purple grapes and a chunk of what appeared to be hard cheese wrapped in a cloth. He set the cheese on the ground and held the fruit out to her.

She selected a plump grape off the bunch and then popped it in her mouth, savoring the sweet juices that ran down her throat. She ate a few more, watching him do the same. Each time he bit into one, she surged with lust. Did everything about him have to be sexy?

She cleared her throat. "What problem do you have to work out?"

Darius stiffened and set the remaining fruit down. "I can't say."

"Can't or won't?"

"You are very bold for a woman."

"Do you expect less?"

"No. Not from you. You are different from the women I have met."

"Have you met many?" she whispered. Not that his past love life mattered, but she was a little curious. Especially with what he had to offer and what was about to happen during the night.

"Met many, found none." He met her gaze. "Until you. You confuse me."

"Me?" She giggled. "I'm pretty ordinary."

"Not from my observation." He stared out into the dark night. Had he also been hurt by a lost love?

"You haven't known me very long." She brushed her hair behind her ears.

"And yet it is comfortable to be near you." He placed his hand on her knee and she gasped.

"I am enjoying the evening, too." She shivered.

"Are you cold?" he asked, rubbing her leg.

"Not really." She laid her head on his shoulder. "Why did you ask for this match? And why now?"

He sat up, pulling his hand away and leaving coldness in its wake. He rubbed his temples. "I didn't ask, I agreed. The Sibyl had a vision."

"Oh," she said, pulling away.

"Don't mistake me. I am very glad to be with you. But I don't know what it means."

"But you want this?" Not just a Roman god, but a man with feelings. His face clenched with tension as he scooped up the food, dropped it in the basket then set it aside.

He paused, unmoving. "I've struggled with life's meaning and loneliness." He rubbed his chin and shifted. "This is right. This night. You."

"I don't know what to say." She drew her knees to her chest and hugged them.

"Tell me why *you* are here." He put his palm back on her knee, and she weakened. "Surely I am not the only one with needs."

"I, uh, have some things to work out, too. I need to trust my decisions. Live." She put her hand on his and rubbed with her thumb.

"Yes," he said, staring into the darkness again. "To learn to live. But how?" He turned to her, his gaze blazing through her soul.

She swallowed. Brazen? Or honest? Now or never. "We don't have to talk right now. We can just live."

Chapter Five

Darius sighed. Could this woman be the one to answer his needs—all of them? For now, she offered what he could take tonight without regret. The rest would come. Perhaps the Sibyl's vision had meaning beyond his dreams and he would find his peace. The night was young, but its promise grew full and deep.

Eleanor pressed nearer to him and his loneliness tore at him like a viper's bite in his groin. Could she sate his need and his loneliness? His body ripened with the possibility. She nestled against him. So warm.

"I want to leave behind the day's responsibilities."

"I want to exist in this moment and forget the past for now." She blinked. "Is that possible?"

"Possible, and desirable." His cock surged. It would take great restraint to hold back his urgent need. The night held so many prospects, and he had to pace himself.

"Okay, then let's live now. No more excuses," she whispered.

Not needing another cue, he reached for her, feeling her flesh give under his fingers as he grasped her soft arms. She moaned so softly that he wasn't sure he heard her. He rose on his knees and drank her in, her lids fluttering half closed as she offered her moist mouth to him. Patience. She was his to pick. "You are so beautiful," he said. "Fortune has smiled on me."

She ducked her head and he tipped her chin back up so that her gaze met his.

"Look at me," he whispered. "Don't shy away from me now."

She nodded her assent.

He ran his thumb across her cheek and down her jaw, tracing the skin all the way to where her neck met her shoulders. He pushed her hair away and admired the gentle slope of her neck. Her pale skin gave under the pressure of his thumb. So soft. He couldn't wait any longer.

He put one hand on the back of her head, and then leaned in for a kiss. As their lips met, she whimpered and he slipped his tongue into her open mouth. She met it with her own, tasting of sweetness and grapes. His mind reeled. She did not back down but met him as an equal. Lust filled him like a rush of heat from a billowing fire.

A night hawk squalled close by and he paused for a second then he lost himself in the kiss. He ran his fingers through her long hair. Her response was not timid, but bold and exploring. She didn't wait for him to initiate contact, but met him with need. He lingered, wanting to savor every stroke of her tongue against his.

Finally, she broke the kiss, gasping. He held her at arm's length, taking in her features. Her face flushed and her forehead dampened with dewy perspiration. So beautiful. Her eyes blazed with desire. No turning back.

He laid her flat onto the blanket, and then covered her with his body and put his head on her chest. She held his head, stroking his hair, and he listened to her heart beating. The rush of water beside them and the quiet whisper of leaves in the wind lulled him. He wasn't a senator, he was a man. His cares slipped downstream.

He sat back. Eleanor's hair fanned around her head and the warm light of the oil lamp colored her in a golden glow. He trailed a fingertip down her chest to her stomach. She stifled a laugh, then sat and wrestled her shirt over her head and tossed it aside. She had a smaller shirt on underneath and in a moment, it was gone, too. He inhaled. She crossed her arms over her breasts and looked at him, mouth parted slightly.

"This is what you want?" he whispered.

She nodded.

He tugged at his belt then released his tunic and stood, stripping bare. Stretching his arms skyward, he begged the gods to give him patience.

Eleanor stared. He was a god and this had to be a dream. He stretched above her, his form hard and strong. She wanted to reach out to his erect cock and it bobbed, but bravery escaped her. She'd never been so bold. Wetness seeped into her underwear. She trembled at the thought that he would soon be in her.

"We, uh, need a condom," she said, reaching into her pocket and pulling out the packet.

"What?" He put his hands on his hips and stared down at her.

"Protection," she said. "Your Sibyl friend certainly left the cave prepared. These were in the box." She held up the condom.

Her hands shook as she opened the packet and he shuddered at her inadvertent touch as she put the condom on him.

"I've never seen a sheath like that before." He stroked himself. "It's thin."

She shrugged. How was she supposed to respond to that comment? At least Madame Eve, or the Sibyl, had provided for the rendezvous. She didn't carry a condom and Darius had no place to put one, not like a toga had pockets. She giggled. This role-playing was becoming quite the turn-on.

"Do I look funny?" he asked, wiggling his hips and swaying his cock.

She slipped out of her shorts and underwear, tossed them off the blanket, and then lay back, gazing up at the starry sky. Passion burned her from within, and she ached to feel his touch. She held her arms out to him.

He was on her quickly, seeking every yielding bit of flesh. He nipped and sucked at her neck and collarbone until she felt like she would collapse for lack of breath. She pushed against him, needing to feel his rough kisses. When he didn't take her breasts in his mouth, she held his head to them and he looked up to her for permission then buried his head and sucked one nipple to tautness then the other. Her hips bucked, seeking an end to his torture of her chest, but he didn't stop.

When she couldn't take any more teasing and forced his head away, he stopped and lay full against her, his hard cock resting on her thighs. She moaned. Over his shoulder, the moon watched from the dark sky. Could the night get any better?

He raised up over her, obscuring the moon.

She spread her legs to give him access, and he groaned as his cock touched her warmth.

She reached for him. As he entered her, she lifted her hips and stifled a groan. A perfect fit.

He held himself up by his arms and lay still, eyes closed. She encouraged him to move and his eyes flew open. She gasped at the need that shone in them. He thrust forward and lay on her, brushing her hair away from her cheeks, and then he kissed her softly, his tongue moving in her mouth.

Her hips rocked against him again. His cock throbbed inside her and she put her hands on his ass and pulled him deeper.

He groaned and the world disappeared in a rush of desire and excitement as he thrust into her again and again until she came in great spasms mixed with his own release.

The world came back in bits–first sounds and rushing water then sight and trees draping above her, barely visible in the dark night. She sighed. He wasn't in her. She closed her eyes again, hoping the dream would return.

"Eleanor," he whispered.

He lay beside her. She turned to face him and shivered. The night air cooled her damp skin.

"I've watched you while you slept. You are made for me."

Ah, the fantasy. If only it were true. She threw her arms around his neck and hugged him, sobbing. The world was cruel with its promises of love. You could never count on passion beyond the moment.

"Have I hurt you?" he asked, hugging her. "I can't bear to think I hurt you."

She sniffled. His hug felt so right and she nuzzled into his neck. "No. You aren't the one who hurt me. You've helped me see that I am desirable and worthy."

"Then why do you cry?"

She sighed. How to explain things without ruining the evening? "I cry because I see that I have not experienced the depth of feeling that I could."

"And that makes you cry?" He held her at arm's length.

"You made me feel special. You showed me there is more to experience and I can't be afraid to take chances. Thank you."

"And you showed me not to give up, either. It isn't too late." He kissed her.

"This night is perfect," she said.

"The night isn't over." He held her to him. "Let's finish dining."

He fed her bits of cheese, feeling her lips with his thumb as she chewed. No woman had ever been so open with him. So honest. But to bring a barbarian back to his house in Rome—the senators would be enraged. It wasn't possible. What was the Sibyl thinking?

No possibility of being together after tonight, though every piece of him wanted her. He sighed and dropped his shoulders. What was he supposed to learn from this test? That what he wanted was unattainable? The Sibyl had already said as much. *No love in his lifetime.*

He put a piece of cheese in his mouth and chewed. Eleanor watched him.

He stood and walked to the edge of the water. It pooled in front of him like a vast black nothingness. Like the future. What would time hold for him?

She slipped her arms around him from behind and rubbed her naked form against his back. Oh, gods, she felt amazing. She laid her head on his back and her hair tickled down to his thighs. He turned and hugged her to his chest. So warm.

"Do you ever wish you could find that one person you could trust and share everything with?"

His breath caught in his throat. Oh, yes. More than she could know. "I do." He lifted her chin. "But is it possible?" he whispered. "So many obstacles."

"I used to believe it." Her eyes filled with tears, and he caught one before it splashed onto her cheek.

He kissed her gently. "Have you been harmed in love?"

"Yes, very much." She wiped her face. "But you made me comfortable. More than I would have expected." She stroked his hair and trailed her fingers down his neck and then his arm.

"And I am comfortable with you."

Holding her was so right. He tried to imagine her with him. She would not be able to live in Rome as his wife. No senator could marry a pale-skinned woman. She trembled.

"Come, let's go back over here and sit. You are cold. I'll get another blanket from the cave."

"Thank you."

He settled her on the ground then made his way to the cave. The moss on the edge of the cave entrance caressed his feet as he walked. It felt so good to be barefoot. He stepped into the cave and grabbed two blankets then picked up the box sitting on the table. After opening it, he saw the row of square packages with sheaths inside. *Peculiar*. He took another one out, set the box down, and headed outside to join her.

She sat bathed in the flickering yellow of the oil lamp, her arms crossed over her chest and her knees drawn up. She smiled as he approached.

"Here you go," he said, draping the blanket around her shoulders.

"Thank you."

He palmed the packet with the sheath and put the extra blanket around him then sat down. "I am thirsty. Are you?"

"Yes."

He set the packet aside and picked up the full decanter. The wine's tartness permeated the air and he took a long drink, splashing it into his mouth and down his throat. Sweet and sour at once, much like life as of late. He lowered the bottle.

"That is good," he said. "Here, I will hold it for you." She pulled the blanket close.

She tipped her mouth up and he poured slowly, flushing at the sight of her drinking the wine. A dribble ran down her cheek and splashed on her neck. She laughed as he bent in to lick it off. "That tickles."

"Let's try this," he said, nipping her on the neck. She arched toward him with a soft groan. He released her then set the wine on the ground and laid her back.

She couldn't place what it was that made Darius feel so right. The brevity of their moment together surely had something to do with it. That, and knowing he wouldn't have a chance to hurt her like Peter had. She stared at him as he crouched over her. He winked. He made her feel like a kid and a woman all at once. She had almost forgotten how hot he was—but not quite.

He pressed his chest against hers then rolled her on top of him, pulling the blanket away so their naked bodies touched. Her hair fell across his face and he moved it away then held her. "Why are you here?" he asked.

"Don't you know? Madame Eve sent me."

"Eve? The Sibyl mentioned her but I do not know who she is." His hand caressed her lower back under the blanket and she shivered. "What does Eve have to do with you?" His touch would never grow old. She sat up, straddling him and smiled as he winced and ground his hips into her.

"Madame Eve set us up to fulfill my request," she said.

"I don't understand what you speak of. What request did you make?"

Eleanor smiled. "She knew just what I needed. I requested a night with a kind man who could make me believe there was hope that I could be desirable and one day, even loved."

"But how? A barbarian can't request any kind of

rendezvous. Even with a prostitute." His hands rested on her hips and he held her in place. He scowled, his face blue in the moonlight.

"I'm no prostitute."

He held her legs with his hands. "I know you are not. I am saying that a barbarian cannot request a prostitute. Or a senator. Yet here I am."

She brushed his cheek, feeling the beginnings of prickly whiskers shadowed along the curve. "I am not a barbarian, either." The pangs of desire stirred again and she rocked against him.

"You say that. So what are you? And how did come to be here?"

"I was in Rome on vacation and I went online to read about sites to see and found her website."

He struggled to sit up and she moved off him. "That's not possible. You could not have been in Rome."

"I was. I made an online request for a match. I didn't know how long it would take and I wasn't really expecting it so soon. I went shopping and found an obscure place where I bought this." She twisted the ring on her finger and he watched her. Was it really his? No, it had to be part of the set up.

"I don't know why my ring would be for sale, but please continue."

"After I made my purchase from the most curious shopkeeper, I went to sit in the Forum. It was so hot and sunny." She closed her hand into a fist and looked at the golden signet gleaming in the moonlight.

"The Forum?" His voice raised an octave. "The Senate would have you stoned!"

She laughed. "No need for this charade. 1Night Stand or not, I don't need to role play. You are perfectly satisfactory without it." She cupped his face.

"What charade? You are lucky to be alive." He

pulled her hands away. "Augustus would have you sentenced to death, or worse."

What the hell was going on? "Augustus is long dead." She scowled.

"Shhh!" he hissed and his body tensed beneath her. "You will get us both killed for speaking of the emperor that way."

The game had gone on long enough. Sure, he was handsome as a Roman god or senator. But things were getting bizarre. "I passed out on the Forum and woke up in the olive grove. But you must know that. It was part of the plan Madame Eve had for us."

"I know nothing of how you got here! I consulted the Sibyl this afternoon. She said I would find you in the grove, as she had seen in a vision. I walked down from the temple and you were there. I didn't question her."

Eleanor shivered, covering her arms with her hands. She surveyed the landscape, trying to find a hint of civilization. No electric lights. No power lines. Darius's toga. No way.

"What year is this?" she asked, afraid to hear the answer. Her heartbeat thudded in her ears.

"The age of Augustus, of course." He shoved her off him and sat up.

"What?" A low, queasy feeling crept into her throat.

"Augustus. Even a barbarian should have heard of him." He stood.

What the hell? She got to her feet to stand beside him and dragged the blanket with her. "That isn't possible."

"Are you ill?" He wrapped an arm around her, and for a moment, she wished it were the truth. She was in Ancient Rome. How perfect would that be? A simpler time and a senator at her side.

"Do you have a car? A flashlight?" She cinched

the cover tight around her.

"I don't know what you mean."

Dizziness overtook her and she swayed. She would not faint again. He scooped her cocooned form into his arms and held her close. "Let's go in the cave where it is warmer. We can talk there."

"My clothes...."

"I'll retrieve them. For now, let's get inside."

No way was she in Ancient Rome. It wouldn't top being in Darius's arms, but seeing the Eternal City when Ovid was alive would be the experience of a lifetime for any student of the classics. She laid her head on his shoulder and he carried her into the small cave.

Chapter Six

Darius shook his head and rubbed his eyes. It could not be true. She could not be from the future. How would that even be possible? Did the gods ever move through time? And what now? Surely the Sibyl knew.

He watched her sleep. He brushed her hair away from the perfect line of her back then traced it with his fingertip. She was so perfect—for him.

The warm humidity of the cave sank into his muscles and he stretched. He could sleep now if it weren't for the problem of Eleanor and her tales of the future. He'd asked her about Rome, and she'd filled him in pretty thoroughly. Either she was the world's best storyteller, or what she said was true. And if so, it explained a lot of things. Her hair, her attitude, and her clothing. She knew Ovid's poetry, and no barbarian would be privy to those verses.

He sighed and stretched out beside her, wrapping his arm around her waist and lying up against her backside. He pulled the blanket up to cover them both. She flipped over and nuzzled under his chin and he kissed the top of her head.

"I can't believe it," she mumbled.

"Me, either." He hugged her.

"What are we going to do?" she asked, wrapping her arms about his midsection.

"It doesn't matter if we are from different times. If that is the case. We have tonight. It isn't enough, but maybe it will last me forever. I will spend my dreams coming back to this moment, even in my old age.

"It doesn't matter tonight. We can worry about tomorrow, tomorrow."

The drumming of the water falling into the pool outside the cave pounded a steady rhythm. He held her tightly and stroked her hair, kissing her forehead. Her response to him had been different than any other woman. She moved with him, not for him. She was smart and funny. Why did she have to be a barbarian from the future?

"What are you thinking about?" She drew away and propped up on her elbow.

"You," he said.

"What about me?"

"I don't want this night to end." He reached for her, lips close.

"Nor do I." she murmured.

"Let's make it worth being here." He took her into a deep kiss. If tonight was all they had, he would make it memorable for both of them.

Darius was perfect. So what if he was really a senator from the time of Augustus? It didn't matter. He felt right. For one night, it didn't matter. Tonight, they had each other.

His rough kiss caught her mid-thought, and she lost her breath for a second. She struggled against him then relaxed as his warm tongue found hers. She joined him, savoring the contact. He kissed at her chin from one ear to the other and she giggled at the tickling. Her nipples stood hard and erect and he grunted as he took one into his mouth. She arched her back and held his head in place and he sucked harder, nipping and lightly biting. Even if he was from the past, he knew how to please a woman.

Her head spun as he trailed his tongue down her stomach, stopping to nuzzle her belly button before spreading her legs and settling his head between them. She tensed, waiting. Her legs quivered when he kissed the inside of each thigh. Damn, it felt so good.

She bucked at the first nip, then she opened her legs and he held them in place as he ran his tongue around her clitoris again and again until she moaned. If only it would never end. The pleasure spiraled out from her core and she bucked against him. He slipped two fingers inside her and pushed and she went over the edge, crying out and not caring who heard her. Her voice rose above the water and he slid them in deeper. She looked down at him, his face near her thighs.

His eyes filled with need and she pushed him back onto his knees as she sat up. She smiled, running her hand down his firm belly and into the dark curls below. His strained for her to touch him and she bent down.

"Is this what you want?" she purred.

"Yesss." He held his erection for her but she bent her head lower, blowing across him.

She placed her hands on his hips and guided him closer to her mouth then stuck out her tongue and licked from underneath his balls up to the head of his cock. He cried out.

"Must you tease me?" His breath rasped.

"I'm not teasing," she said, kissing the moistness off the tip of his erection. The saltiness filled her mouth and she longed for more.

She grasped him and stroked rhythmically, running her tongue over the soft skin. He thrust toward her then began moving in and out of her mouth. She held him, tugging. He stiffened and pushed her away.

"Stop," he whispered. "I can't tolerate this any longer."

"Good," she said. "Let me help you." She took

him in her mouth again and ran her tongue along the underside of his cock.

"No," he groaned. "I want to find my pleasure inside you."

She reached out and cupped his balls. "Okay, I won't complain."

"Let's not forget the sheath," he said. He took out the packet from under the blanket, tore it open, and unrolled it on himself.

She squeezed him, and he surged in her hand. Oh, yes, she was ready to feel him back inside her.

He turned her around on all fours on the pallet and held her hips as he tried to thrust in from behind. She reached down between her legs and guided him to the wet spot and he leaned forward, growling. Eleanor gasped. He was perfect.

Pleasure rippled through her as he pumped in and out and she squeezed her thighs together. He grunted and his strokes became short. She followed him, panting, and the sensation grew until she shuddered with ecstasy. He held still as she came, then thrust a couple of times and released with a guttural groan.

She collapsed on the pallet, trying to catch her breath. He smacked her backside gently then lay down beside her. The sheen of his sweat glistened in the yellow light from the oil lamp. She sighed. Not only did he have a magnificent body, he knew how to use it. Her contentment reached beyond sexual satiety; it filled her emotionally, warming those cold places of doubt and mistrust.

Chapter Seven

Pink shadows of early morning sunlight streaked into the cave and the water's splash resounded with bright new vigor. Darius sat, eating the last of one of the loaves the Sibyl's attendant had packed into the food basket. Eleanor could have bread and a piece of cheese for breakfast, once he got her up. He took a drink of the wine, its warmth searing his throat. The night had been good. It was the best night he had ever shared with a woman.

He yawned. She lay sleeping beside him, her hair covering her face like a golden veil. He watched her back rise and fall with her soft breath. Even now, after a night of passion, he stirred. Never had a woman so captivated him. If only she could be with him every day and night.

Once he woke her, the end would be in sight. They would have to part ways. He didn't want to break the spell, but he soon would have to go back to the reality of being a senator in Rome. Ancient Rome, apparently.

He brushed the crumbs away and stood to dress. The Sibyl had bade him return in the morning, and they needed to get there before the line lengthened with people who held a higher position than he did. Lower men who had waited the night would already be lined up waiting for an audience. Some days it was good to be a senator.

How he would get her into the temple was another matter. She was a woman, and her skin was fair. Perhaps with a disguise he could sneak her in, or pay off the guards. But surely it would not be necessary; the seer would provide for them. She commanded his appearance, after all. He slipped his tunic over his head and straightened then belted it.

The waterfall glistened in the new morning light. He needed to hurry. He checked to make sure all the oil lamps were extinguished then slipped on his shoes. The trek uphill to the temple would be tiring.

After winding his heavy toga onto his shoulders, he bent to wake Eleanor. He hated to have to rouse her. He shook her. She inhaled and stretched, not opening her eyes. He couldn't believe that their time together was nearing an end. How would he ever recover? He shook her again, and then bent to kiss her forehead.

"We must go," he said. "The Sibyl is waiting for us."

"Already?" she murmured. "I am so tired."

"Yes, we have to go."

She moaned. "I want to stay here." She peeked at him.

He smiled then bent to nuzzle her ear. "Me, too. But we cannot keep her waiting."

She flipped onto her back and stretched her arms high. The woolen blanket slipped down and he drank in her curved form and soft breasts.

"You have to get dressed." To wake next to her each morning would be glorious.

She sat up and nodded, her golden hair cascading over her back. She looked like a water nymph perched on a rock, alluring and soft. If she sang to him, he would lose all control, and they would not make it to the Sibyl any time soon. He shook his head. No time for daydreams. They needed to go.

Eleanor gasped. The marble structures perched

on the hill high above the valley sparkled in dawn's pink magnificence. Entirely formed and stately, they stood in contrast to modern Rome's skeletal offerings. She held Darius's hand, and as they grew closer to the Sibyl's temple she pressed in close to him.

"Oh my," she said. "The buildings are amazing. I can't believe I am seeing them in working order."

"Shhh," he whispered. "Don't draw more attention to us. My empire can be very dangerous."

She clutched his arm.

He nodded, directing her to the line that had formed outside. Men stepped out of his way, allowing them to pass, but she heard the mumblings behind them. She was not welcome in this society. Was her life in danger, as he had said?

A chill sliced through her, and he put his arm around her shoulder. She would be okay. As long as he stood beside her, she had nothing to fear.

"Remember, let me talk," he whispered.

She squeezed his hand. Not a problem. What would she say to these ancients anyway? *Thanks for the tour*?

He led her near the front of the line, stepping into place behind one man who was clearly from a wealthy family. The man nodded at Darius then stuck his nose up at her. *Okay, then!*

Soon, they were at the head of the line waiting their turn to go into the temple. A shrill shriek tore over the line. A large hawk strafed the crowd, calling as it flew by. Men ducked and the bird glided past them and toward Eleanor. She froze. It lifted higher, missing her, and then settled on top of the temple, screeching.

Someone behind her said, "It's an omen. Beware."

She shuddered. The bird stared at her. What did

it want?

The guards motioned them to the door. "Go ahead, Senator."

They moved toward the door, and one of the guards held out his hand. "She cannot enter."

"I say she enters with me on the Sibyl's command," Darius growled.

"As you wish, Senator," the smaller guard squeaked, stepping aside.

The men shook their heads and waved them inside. They respected power. *Thank goodness.*

Her pulse surged in the cool darkness.

"I'm scared," she whispered. "I don't want us to be apart."

"I have faith that the Sibyl will know what is best for us." He hugged her to him. "No matter what, I will never forget you."

"Or me, you." Tears formed and she pushed them back.

She fingered the ring. Soon, she would have to return it to its owner and keep only memories. If only real life could be so—real.

This fantasy was about to end. At least she had found someone and something so much more powerful than her thin memory of Peter. The one-night stand had served its purpose and she would never settle for less than she deserved again. The senator had made his mark on her heart forever.

***

"Darius," the Sibyl hissed. "You return." Incense smoke filled the chamber, mixed with the gasses of the cave. How the seer stayed down here for any length of time was a mystery.

"I do." He squeezed Eleanor's clammy hand. She must be terrified.

"And you brought the woman, Eleanor."

"Yes, she has come with me. I found her in the olive grove as you said. We thank you for the accommodation in the cave." How much did the seer know?

"And your night...was it satisfactory?" He could have sworn the Sibyl smiled, but her piles of wrinkles covered all but the strongest emotions.

He blushed. "Very much so." He wasn't used to discussing his intimate business.

"And, how about you, Eleanor? Did you find your night satisfactory?"

"Y-yes."

"I see." The old woman stood and crept toward them in the dim half-light. "Now is a time of choice. Darius, will you return to the Senate?"

"I don't want to. I want to stay at her side but she cannot go to Rome. Are there other choices?"

"And what do you wish, Eleanor?"

"I wish to be with him. But I can't stay here, my life will be threatened. I don't look like everyone else."

The Sibyl laughed, and then cackled. The vibrations echoed throughout the cave and Eleanor leaned on Darius. A large hawk shrieked and landed on the floor beside the seer. How did a bird get into the lower cave?

With a great flapping of wings, the bird disappeared, and a man stood in its place. The Sibyl put her arm around him.

"Don't you know what to do?" she asked.

"No." Darius said, holding Eleanor. Who was this man? Was he here to take her away? "What *can* we do?"

"I think you know, my dear," the old man said to Eleanor. "You still have the ring?"

"Yes," she breathed, holding it up to show him.

"How did you get here?" She turned to Darius. "He's the shopkeeper who had your ring."

"I don't understand," he replied.

"Go together into Eleanor's time," the Sibyl hissed. "Eve sees your happiness in the future."

Darius's heart skipped. Could he do that? Leave everything he had worked to build here? Yes, those things were replaceable. But to go into the future? "Is that possible?"

"Anything is possible," the shopkeeper said. "Hasn't Eve shown you that?"

Darius iced. *You will not find love in your lifetime.* The words' meaning opened to him. Why had he not realized it before now? Not in *his* lifetime, but in Eleanor's. He would find love. He had found love. "Do you wish me to join you?"

She smiled. "Yes! Let's live in my time. You will be relieved of your burdens here. You can even run for Senator back home if you want." Her eyes sparkled. She held up her hand with his golden signet on her finger. He chuckled and clasped her hand then leaned in for a kiss as the world gave way beneath their feet.

Druid, Mine

Book 2

Dedication

To my Prince....

Druid, Mine

Anya's wish for a normal date—away from the old man she is caretaker for—comes true in unexpected ways when she finds herself whisked to an ancient Irish stone circle on solstice eve.

Carrick's decision to follow the path to become an Ovate druid has not come lightly, and he plans to spend the solstice eve in meditation unless fairies or evil spirits disrupt the circle. When a feisty girl walks right up to the fire, more than sparks fly.

They each seek healing and a connection, but the darkness of summer is short, and once the solstice sun breaks through the circle at dawn, the magic of the night will be over. Even Madame Eve can't stop the day from rising.

Chapter One

"Another?" the bartender asked. He ran his hand through his tousled pale hair and flashed an *I'm available* smile.

"No, I'd better call it a night." Anya turned from his gaze while heat rose in her cheeks. He was always so forward. What didn't he understand about no? "I'll take my check." She pushed her empty glass across the bar toward him. "Please." She wiped her fingertips on the bar napkin and then spread it back out into a neat square in front of her. The bartender didn't move, but watched her intently.

"It's early. Sure you don't want another pint? You've only had one. Got your favorite Irish brew on tap." His arm brushed hers then crept over to full contact. "Me."

A shiver raced through her. Could he be the one Madame Eve had chosen? A man right under her nose? His crookedly handsome grin—the same one she had seen every Saturday night she'd been coming into the little Irish pub in the North Carolina mountains—grew larger. She jerked her arm away. *Don't think so.* "I've got to go."

"If you say so, honey." He paused and trailed a finger across the bar, nearly, but not touching her. She wished she had worn more than a low-cut sundress. The air vibrated with the hum of a dozen conversations and though the bar was almost full, she sat alone. Again. He smirked. "Right back with your bill. You have time to change your mind." He grabbed the heavy pint glass and spun away.

Anya sighed and rubbed her arm, trying to quiet the sensations boiling inside her. Great. She'd managed to piss off the one guy who had paid any attention to her in a long time. Why was single life so complicated? The bar was filled with individuals who apparently wanted to stay that way—they came every Saturday, looking for a hookup. They'd be back the next week, hoping for another distraction. Few ever returned with the same person. Was she destined for that same hollow existence? Maybe Madame Eve would get her over the hump, so to speak.

The one established couple in the bar leaned in close across one of the small tables, whispering. No doubt planning their lives and sharing dreams. The woman giggled, her hair falling over her face as she laughed. The man smiled a Hollywood smile then tucked her hair behind her ears. Anya turned away. It was worse than a soap opera.

The bartender swooped up behind her and pressed against her back.

"Here you go," he whispered, dropping the check over her shoulder onto the bar.

He was gone before she could protest.

Oh crap!

Her heart pounded. *I never checked in.* How long had it been? Standing, she searched her purse for her smartphone and found it buried in the bottom. Relieved, she unlocked the phone and checked her messages. *What if....*

"Oh." *I forgot. Mr. Mitchell is gone for the week.* With his niece to New York. The boss had actually taken a vacation without her and she wasn't at his beck and call. For a whole week. And there she sat at her usual spot, already done with her beer and it was barely seven p.m.

Tossing the phone back into her purse, she pulled out a credit card and set it on the receipt.

Loser. No wonder I'm single.

The bartender scooped up her card. Maybe she should learn to compromise. Accept less. She certainly wasn't finding the perfect lover or soul mate with an all-day and truly all-the-time job.

The clinking of glasses and an occasional belt of laughter in the pub usually comforted her with some semblance of belonging. Loneliness pooled in her stomach. Normally, she'd get a couple hours off on the weekend and come for a few drinks, but then it'd be back to the mansion to be there when the old man woke up. His care had become mostly around the clock with few breaks when someone else filled in. Tonight, she didn't have to go back. Maybe she'd get a hotel room. Live it up. Order room service instead of being a short order cook. For now, she was alone.

"Here you go." The bartender set her card and receipt on the bar. "Will my favorite hot redhead be back next week? Or is that old man going to keep her all to himself?"

She scowled. "Got a pen?"

For a moment she considered inviting him to meet her after his shift. What was the harm? He was handsome, if a bit gangly. Clearly he had high self-esteem. But then there would be that awkward moment the next time she wanted to come in the pub for a beer, and he'd be grinning like the cat that ate the canary. No, not a good idea. Better to have a fling with a stranger than someone she'd have to see again.

He pulled a pen from his apron and gripped it when she tried to take it. He smiled before finally letting it go. *Jerk.* Leaving him a tip as always, she grabbed her purse and headed out the door, storming past the lovebirds that were now feeding each other French fries. *Ugh.*

The warm air was typical midsummer mountain weather—sticky until the breeze pushed through. She pulled at her pale blue dress and fanned it out to cool off. Her small purse dead weighted across her shoulder and her sandals begged to be ditched, but the cobblestone streets of Ardale were likely filthy with who-knew-what refuse from the summer partying. Music thumped from the alleyways between buildings and groups of people gathered in doorways and at the street-side tables, hoping to make a connection for the evening. The sun had barely dipped below the horizon and people were on the prowl. The heavy stench of beer and cigarettes hung in the air, mixed with too many kinds of perfume and aftershave. She stepped out into the street, gazing up the road at the row of bars. Each one held possibility. Or ruin.

The town had transformed into quite the place for parties. Old man Mitchell had been her charge for so long that her forays into town on the weekends pretty much meant dinner and a beer, but she'd seen the trend toward more fun and wilder times. With the rare vacation, she could sample what the town had to offer. Alone. She glanced over her shoulder at the heavy wooden door of the pub. The bartender would join her later, if she asked him. In all the months she'd been stopping in, she'd never asked his name. Sighing, she walked away.

Heading up the narrow street, she strolled along the bumpy stones that hadn't seen car traffic in many years. Once the town became a tourist destination, the council tried to do anything to lure businesses into the city hub and pull in revenue and more people. *Looks like it worked.* Gas streetlights lit the street and the shadows flickered across gaggles of people gathering in youthful celebration of a week's end. The latest fashion was to wear anything in the closet from the past fifty years, and then add old sneakers or boots. She shook her head and headed up the hill to the end of the street, ignoring the rising conversation and occasional catcall around her.

The street curved up to the city's center—a roundabout pedestrian mall circling a tall, rocky fountain with benches around its perimeter. At the top of the fountain perched a statue of a fairy, trailing a garland of stone roses from her hands and down into the basin. Blue-green lights shone on the statue, bending rainbows of mist around the entire fountain. The falling water splashed in thick summer air. *My favorite place to sit and think.*

She yawned. The mall lay mostly quiet around her, with only the scratch of a skateboard on concrete somewhere in the distance. A few couples blended into the background around the area, but most had sought out more privacy than the promenade provided. *Thank goodness.*

She pulled her knees up to her chin and wrapped her arms around them. Why couldn't her own life be normal? Getting mixed up with Mr. Mitchell had been sketchy at best, but it provided a great income, and she certainly never needed anything. Except human contact. That's what had spurred the 1Night Stand idea on in the first place. She'd seen the website late one night while online in her room at the old man's mansion. It had taken over a month to even revisit the site and then another six weeks to make the decision that it was the right thing to do. Three weeks later and she still waited for her match, and doubts were growing. What if there wasn't anyone out there who wanted to be with her? *Maybe I'm the first person Madame Eve can't find a match for.* And how was it any better than just picking someone up from one of the dozen bars along the street?

Bile filled her throat. Being caretaker for the old man had filled her days but left her empty inside. *I'm lonely. I need this 1Night Stand.* She stifled a sob. Crying wouldn't help anything. She had chosen her path knowing full well what the consequences would be. Maybe she hadn't foreseen how deeply alone she'd feel, but she'd known what she was getting into, work-wise. She used to be a risk taker, impulsive and willing to try new things. Why was she so willing to settle for security now?

The town's few buildings rose in shadowed relief in the dusky twilight around the city center like tall stones. Guardians, perhaps. Behind them lay the mountains, the wild unknown. She sat straight and leaned into the faint spray from the fountain. The cool mist spread across the back of her arms. Closing her eyes, she lifted her long hair so the moisture could reach the back of her neck.

"Aine?"

Anya dropped her hair.

"Hello?" *No one.*

"Aine. Let's go." The voice floated on drops of water and fell through the air.

"What?" No one was near.

"I'm here." The voice settled softly like dew on her skin. The air wavered over the fountain and the water slowed.

I only had one beer.

"Come. He awaits."

For the briefest moment, a golden light eclipsed the edge of Anya's vision then darkness slid over her.

Chapter Two

Carrick paced beside the hearth fire. The dark sky domed overhead and light from the crescent moon flecked the stones of the Grange circle around him. Where was Torin? The lad was always late. He stopped and stomped his foot, his shoe kicking up a cloud of dirt. The fire couldn't be properly guarded until the herbs were burning. Fay were likely already scampering about inside the circle readying mischief on this midsummer's eve. Torin should have arrived before the moon reached the treetops.

Waves of heat rolled off the hearth in the grassy center of the stone circle. The flames swayed and danced in the light breeze lifting off Loch Gair, but beads of sweat still rolled down his back in a slow trickle. He patted his damp tunic against his back then flung a branch onto the blaze. Soon enough the mist would creep in from the lake and cool the land, but at the moment, the day's warmth still spread out along the hillside and into the slight dip where the stone circle lay. Raising his arms above his head, he stretched.

He drank from his water skin. Torin could ruin the whole ritual if he didn't arrive soon. Star blossoms overflowed from a large basket that sat near his blanket, and he grabbed handful of the pungent flowers. Tossing them into the air above the flames, he watched them float down and wink out as they burned. When gathered near solstice, the flowers kept evil spirits away, and the youth of the village had gathered enough to burn through the night.

A rustling of leaves caught his attention on the east side of the circle and he spun to a defensive position, his heart pounding. What creature disturbed the holy circle after sundown on this night? Fay or foe? He snatched a large stick from the pile of firewood and brandished it.

Torin sprinted past the towering entry stones, carrying a large pottery crock.

"I worried." Carrick dropped the stick and took the vessel from him. "You are late. The moon has risen over the loch."

"Ovate," the boy panted. "Forgive me. The mead was not ready."

He set the heavy vessel on the ground, the mead sloshing inside. "I'm not Ovate yet. Not until after *Samhuinn* rites."

Torin stood tall for a young boy, but gangly, like he'd been taken apart and put back together in an approximation of himself. His rusty hair held just enough curl to be unmanageable. He fumbled in his belt.

"Here are the herbs." He threw the tied linen roll to Carrick. "You'll soon be Ovate, healer among men. Then you can travel time. Perhaps even talk to your parents." He wiped his brow.

Carrick scowled and waved the packet of herbs in front of him. "An Ovate's life is secret, with no place in time. And my family is dead. The king spilled their blood across the hillside. I have no one. Once I am Ovate, I belong to the Earth forever." He dropped the herbs onto the ground beside the pottery. "You, friend, had well forget me."

"Your foul disposition isn't one I cherish being around tonight." Torin tugged at his short tunic. "It's wise that the initiates tend the Solstice fires. You have time to think about your path and its direction. I'll be on my straw mattress and not on a pile of blankets on damp ground. I don't envy you."

"My duty is to the hearth flame, not a mattress. Tomorrow, when the sun blazes through the stones, I will know I am closer to my legacy. A solitary existence." A few sparks rose into the sky and he watched them dissipate. Had he made the right choice? A low whistle sounded through the trees, barely audible over the crackling flames. *Fay*. Already afoot and causing mischief.

Torin froze. "The fay are out!"

"So it appears."

"Maybe Aine will come to you in the night. Solstice is her night. And you need company. One would hope only the good spirits will visit."

"No fairy queen would want to lie with the likes of me. I fear my days of finding a woman to share my life with have rushed by like a late summer windstorm."

"Bitter as bad mead, you are." Torin kicked the ground with the toe of his boot. "It's no wonder you never found a wife."

"Go. I must tend to my duties."

"The Grange is a magical place. Loch Gair cradles its mysteries."

"It holds its secrets for better men than me."

"Keep your eyes open and your back to the fire." Torin tightened his belt.

"Run swiftly, friend. Lest a fay overtake you."

He dashed out of the circle and Carrick scowled. What was done, was done. It was too late to find a wife—the Ovate initiation had seen to that. Not that it mattered. Death lay everywhere in the green land, and it was best not to care too deeply for anyone, lest they be stolen away or cut down. He sat on the warm stone hearth and tossed blades of grass into the fire, watching them flare briefly before winking out. What was the point of loving someone only to lose them?

The whistling began again, carrying over the stones and around the circle in a whirlwind of sound. A high pitch at first, it quickly dropped to a low moan. He stood. Nothing. No one was near.

He walked to the inside edge of the circle and put his hands on one of the cool stones. The low moan grew deeper. Checking the side of each stone, whether large or small, he found nothing. No animal, no person, no fay.

The moan became a shrieking wail. Covering his ears, he winced. Where was the sound coming from?

"Who is there? What do you want?"

The shrieking faded to a low hum and he uncovered his ears. *Fay, indeed.*

"Carrick." The woman's whisper lingered on the breeze.

Did he imagine it?

"Carrick."

"What? Where are you?" Nothing but countryside spread out beyond the circle.

"I am here." Her voice echoed from stone to stone. "Can you not see me?"

Nothing. Where was she?

"Here," she laughed.

He spun in the direction of the voice but saw only a tall gray stone and empty ground. A faint glow shimmered from the stone's edge, wavering like a hundred dancing fireflies. *Magic.*

"No need to fear, Ovate," she said, stepping from behind the stone. "I have come to help you."

The fay was near normal in human height, and not especially attractive. If she had not had the glowing aura, he'd never have suspected her a fay at all. Her brown locks curled and hung low to her waist and she wore a circlet of fresh roses in her hair.

She motioned him near.

Backing away, he fought the urge to run. If he could get back to the solstice fire, it would protect him from any magic the fay could unleash. *I wish I had worn an amulet.*

"Don't go!"

"You cannot be in the circle. I order you to leave."

"But I have a message for you. And a question." Her voice splashed over him like fresh water scented with sweet roses.

"No tricks! Who are you?" He raised his hands to defend himself. Could she really be dangerous? *My hands are no match for fey magic.*

"My name is Danu." The creature stepped toward him. "Come here. I will explain everything. You have nothing to fear."

He froze. If he didn't obey, what would happen? Would she change him into a suckling pig? And if he took her hands, would she ever let go?

The wind picked up and rushed about him, swirling around his feet and sweeping across his face. Mist had settled thickly over the green land and obscured most things beyond the rim of the circle of stones. The night hung heavy, like a pendulum, everything swaying. What magic was afoot? He clutched his head to steady his vision, but the world continued to bob.

Danu smiled. He clasped her small hands in his own. Her energy passed into him like a streak of fire.

What started with a swirling wind threatened to knock him off his feet. She laughed like rushing water, and he drowned in the dizziness that overtook him.

"Let go of your fear. I will not hurt you."

The world around him slowed as she pulled him closer. "You are unhappy. I have come to help." She reached to stroke his hair.

"Did Torin send you? This is not a night for jokes." He blinked away the lightheadedness that filled him.

"Torin ran from the hill as if a pack of wild beasts chased him," she giggled. "He knows nothing of this."

"Then why are you here?"

"Your family's blood spreads over the land."

"This I know, all too well."

"And you are lonely."

He tried to pull free, but she drew him closer.

"Listen to me! We have watched you. You are a good man. Ovate is an admired position. But you must be sure it is what you truly seek." Her face, symmetrical and pure, was inches from his.

"Ovate is my calling. Time has left me without family or a wife and I have no other choice."

Danu smiled. "Perhaps. But what is the harm in one more night to make sure that you wish to complete your existence alone?"

"What?"

"One more night to make sure you want to be alone forever." Her warm breath tickled his cheek. "You must trust me."

He squirmed. "What are you offering? Surely you don't mean...."

She laughed and the hair rose on his arms. "No, not me. Eve has chosen someone for you—if you accept. For the night. Solstice eve is magical."

"Who is Eve?" He leaned back, but Danu didn't let go.

"Someone who cares."

"It is dangerous to care."

"Yet, she does."

"No."

"Are you sure?" She squeezed. "One night."

"I am no longer a man. I am druid. Ovate."

"Not yet. Give thought to the idea before you

refuse. It might be your last chance to hold a woman in your arms, like this." Danu slid against him. She wrapped her arms around his neck. "Are you sure you are ready to give this feeling up forever? This intimacy?"

Heat rushed through him. He tried to move away but she held on.

"Just one night? Are you certain?" she whispered.

Was he? One night, the solstice eve—he wasn't full Ovate yet. As long as there was no commitment, why not?

"I don't know this Eve. Is she fay?"

"She is someone who wants to help you." Danu's laughter rang over the stones. "If you say yes. You do have a choice."

Who was he to tell a fay no? What harm could come from one night of passion? His last night, ever. Then he could focus on his duties.

"Yes."

"Very well."

He moved to kiss her, but she melted into the air and disappeared on the wind.

***

Anya blinked. The sky was dark. Really dark with zillions of stars. Had she hit her head? She clutched her purse and stood, brushing loose grass off her arms and sundress. *Where the hell am I?*

The grassy hill had a few tall hardwood trees and overlooked a sparkling lake, which curled around the land in a horseshoe. The reflected moonlight cast the lake in a sheen of silver and heavy mist crept along the ground. *This must be a dream.*

Where would the dream take her? Was she asleep at the old man's mansion? Or in a hotel? A brisk wind flirted by and billowed her dress around her legs. She shivered. *Cold dream.* Why didn't she ever have a coat in her dreams?

"Hello?" No answer.

In the distance to her right, a fire burned. *Someone must be tending it.* She walked through the low misty grass toward the blaze. A row of stones lay in her path and she followed along them, around a circle. A low whistle blew through the sparse trees and she shivered. *I hope this dream doesn't turn into a nightmare.* She rubbed her arms, wishing she carried something more menacing than a phone and a credit card. *Next dream, coat and gun.*

Had she had more to drink than she thought? She plucked a yellow, star-shaped flower and twirled it in her fingertips. St. John's Wort? It bloomed all around her, its woody stems climbing and drooping over the misty meadow grass. She tossed the flower aside.

A gap in the stones formed a doorway of sorts, with one opening that appeared to be an entrance. Kind of like Stonehenge without the henges. Anya pinched herself. *Ouch! I thought you didn't feel pain in a dream.*

Maybe this was some kind of joke. Maybe the bartender drugged her then dropped her off in an empty field because she wouldn't go out with him. Then where was he? No, that was ridiculous. *I watch too many cop shows.*

"Hello?" she repeated. She stepped between the tall boulders and a rush of icy air brushed past her. The mist lay heavy on the ground outside the stone circle, but the inside was clear and grassy. Turning, she saw the man sitting by the fire, his back to her.

She didn't want to startle him, but she had to find out where she was and what had happened. Creeping forward, she stumbled. Her heart thudded, and adrenaline surged through her. *This dream could go really wrong about now.*

"Excuse me."

The man turned then headed toward her. She gasped. He was magnificent. Normally, she'd be afraid, but this was a dream and she'd picked a handsome stranger to play her counterpart. He came at her like a panther, his shoulder-length hair falling around his strong face. She took a step backward, sure she looked like a frightened child.

"Who are you?" His skin was as pale as moonlight, and his blue gaze froze her in her tracks. She couldn't speak. Why did it always happen in her dreams?

"Who are you? Who sent you?" he repeated. He looked her up and down.

She stuttered. The man, in his odd tunic, sitting in the middle of nowhere, wanted to know who *she* was? *It's my dream.* "Uh...."

"No more fay tricks." He grabbed her by the shoulders. "Who are you?"

She trembled. "No tricks, I promise." His shoulders were wide and muscular, but not too much so. Exactly like she would dream them. "I'm Anya."

He stumbled back. "What? What did you say your name was?"

"Anya." She shrugged. "Who are you?"

"Carrick."

His tunic, off white and roughly sewn, sat on his body a little sideways. Usually her dreams were a bit more precise. *Must be the beer.* "Good to meet you, Carrick."

"More fay tricks. I have work to do."

Wait a minute, this is my dream.

"Wait. I need help. I'm not sure why I'm here, and I don't even know where I am." She followed him toward the hearth.

He grabbed a small branch off the wood pile and tossed it on the blaze. "Well, go back to where you came from, then. I'm busy."

"I don't know how. I think I'm dreaming. I was sitting by a fountain and this voice spoke to me...."

He turned and she stopped speaking. His blue gaze seared into her.

"Did Eve send you, Aine?"

"Madame Eve?" *Oh my gosh. In a dream? How would that work?*

"Eve. Did the fay send you?" He stepped closer. "Answer me."

Tears spilled down her cheeks. What on earth was wrong with her? She had asked for this. "I don't know. Where am I?"

"You are in the Grange circle. Why do you cry? Do you not wish to be here?"

"I...I...don't know. This must be a dream, because I was sitting in town and now I'm out in the country.... And yes, Madame Eve must have sent me here...." She buried her face in her hands and sobbed.

***

Why was the woman crying? He wasn't much of a caretaker, though his heart heaved to comfort anyone in pain. What should he do?

Pushing her red hair out of the way, he placed a hand on her slender shoulder. When she shuddered at his touch, he squeezed. "Don't cry," he said softly. "You don't have to be here if you don't wish to. It is your choice."

"But I chose to be here. Well, I chose Madame Eve's service."

"Then why do you cry?" What trick had the fay played on him? He'd expected someone more willing to be with him.

"I'm sorry." She wiped her eyes. "I've just had a rough time lately. I'm not usually so weepy."

"I understand." But he didn't. He hadn't seen a woman cry in a long time.

Doubt clouded her gaze, and he tried to reassure her with a smile, but she turned away.

"Come sit on my blankets and I will get you some water. Everything will be fine."

"Okay, thank you." She attempted a smile. The breeze lifted her hair off her shoulders and trailed it across her face. He smiled back.

"I need to finish my work first, but it will only take a moment. Come on."

He placed a large log on the fire. Untying the herb pack, he unrolled it. Muttering a few sacred words, he sprinkled the herbs onto the flames and stared into the black sky. The night was definitely not going along as planned. He peeked at Aine but avoided eye contact.

"Come on." He led her to his blankets on the ground and she sat, her blue dress pooling out around her slim ankles. Her pale skin glowed from within—surely she was fay. And she shared the name of the fairy queen herself. That was no coincidence.

He cleared his throat. "Water or mead?"

"I had enough beer already tonight. No telling where I would end up if I had more." She laughed and the sound poured over him and sent his heart racing. She was lovely.

He handed her the waterskin. When she stared at it oddly, he held it to her lips as she drank.

"Thank you." She ducked her head. "Everything here is so different and strange. You said we are in the Grange circle? That sounds like Ireland. But that isn't possible. What is the name of the curved lake down below the stones?"

"The loch?" He uncorked the mead and took a

long sip. "That is Loch Gair. Ireland? You are in Hibernia, as the Romans call it. We call it Eire, miss."

Her mouth opened to speak, but she uttered no words. Instead, she stood and gazed out over the hillside, past the stones for a moment.

When she turned to him, she almost whispered. "Yes, Madame Eve has sent me here to you. I've come a long way."

The breeze tugged at her dress and tossed her fiery hair about her shoulders. She appeared as a fairy queen, ready to rule her kingdom.

"You wish to be here?"

"This is not what I expected."

"Nor I. The fairy queen doesn't often stoop to visit a lowly druid." He took another drink of mead. *That trickster, Danu.* Solstice eve was never as it seemed.

Anya snorted. "I am no more a fairy queen than you are a druid." She grabbed her purse. "Yet here we are in some wild countryside in a circle of stones and mist rolling around on the hills. I don't know what's going on."

"If you are not fay, then how can you be here?" He stood. "This circle is magic, and fay told me you were coming. Why don't you believe?" He reached for her hand and she pulled away. "You must be here for a reason."

"This place is lovely, I'll agree." She walked and he followed. "But magic? Not so sure I believe in magic anymore. And who is Fay?"

"Fairy folk." *Danu is laughing at me, of that I am sure.*

"Uh, huh. Fairies. The only fairy I've seen lately was part of a fountain. A statue."

"If fay didn't bring you, how did you get here? Where did you come from?"

"Ardale, North Carolina. No idea how I got here.

I heard this woman speaking to me then I fainted or something. Beer, exhaustion, I really don't know what happened."

"I've never heard of North Carolina," he said. "But if you are truly not fay, you must be from another time. No woman would wear such a...." He gulped. "Dress. Not here. Not in this time. Women cover themselves. And your shoes... they are different."

"So you think I'm from another time?" She laughed.

"Druids believe in movement through time, so I think the fay brought you here."

Her smile disappeared. She shook her head. "Well, I'm not a druid."

"I am." He tried to walk beside her but she moved faster.

Reaching the edge of the circle, she said, "Maybe it would make sense, if I believed in that sort of thing. I just don't know. You certainly don't appear to be from modern times."

"Modern?"

"Yes, you know, airplanes and cell phones?" She sighed and tension crossed her face for an instant, like a brief war-cry on a quiet battlefield.

"I don't know what you speak of, but I can tell you are unhappy with your 'modern times'." He waited for a sign of acknowledgement, but she remained still.

"Isn't everyone carrying pain?" Their gazes locked, and for a second, a spark fluttered inside him. A connection. She looked away.

"Yes, everyone. We all have pain. No matter where we stand in time."

She sat on one of the rocks and watched the sky. Her long white neck lay bare and heat filled his groin. Oh, how he wanted to take her pain away, even for only a night. *Even if she is fay. Even if she will be gone tomorrow.*

"I will be back in a moment," he mumbled. "Will you remain here until I return?"

"I don't have anywhere else to go," she sighed.

He touched her knee and she flinched, but didn't move away. "I am glad you are here. I am happy to share the eve instead of spending it alone."

She didn't respond, but a blush crept up her neck and over her cheeks. He left to tend the fire.

***

Anya leaned her head back to watch the stars again. *What is going on?* She swung her feet to and fro. *Not drunk or dreaming. Carrick's real.* He was obviously either some backwoods guy with some weird habits, or some neo-druid who took things a bit too seriously. And how did she get to Ireland? *Or wherever I am. My phone!* She could check her location anywhere in the world with the GPS app.

She searched for her phone. No signal and the battery was almost dead. Fantastic. The extended battery should last two days with moderate use. Didn't Ireland have cell towers? *Dammit!* She tossed the phone back then snapped the bag shut. *If I am really in Ireland, the cell reception sucks.*

Even over the mist, there were no manmade lights at all in the dark countryside. She shivered. The lake reflected the moon and sky. Only the fire in the center of the stone circle was manmade. *Shit!*

Could she have dreamed up a sexier man? Or a nicer one? *Crazy!* Either she was having the most bizarre dream ever, or something really strange was going on. She didn't know where to go or what to do even if she did want out.

The cold stone chilled her backside, and she

shifted her weight. She set her purse beside her and breathed deeply, in and out, trying to relax. What were the options? The breeze rustled. She pulled her knees to her chest and wrapped her arms around them. Coolness seeped into the evening. *It's going to be a long night.*

"Aine?" a voice trickled.

Anya pushed her hair out of her face. "What?"

"Aren't you happy to be here?"

"Show yourself. I want answers." Nothing.

"Here I am, silly." A young woman, slightly glowing, stepped from behind the stone. "But I must hurry."

"What the hell is going on?" She hopped down and approached the woman. "Am I in Ireland? For real?"

"You requested Eve's help. She has granted you your wish. Not in your time, but in a time where a match was found. And yes, in the land you now know as Ireland."

"How is that possible?" Anya crossed her arms.

"Don't you feel the magic in this stone circle here at the Grange? The air hums with possibility—relax and let yourself feel it."

"But I didn't expect...."

"Life doesn't always bring us what we expect now, does it, Aine? The most important thing is for you to trust. Not be so judgmental. You must open yourself to new possibilities." The woman smiled and the breeze swirled around Anya.

"Aine?" Carrick called. "Are you hungry?"

"I must go now," the woman said. "You won't see me until tomorrow. Trust Carrick—he needs you. And trust yourself." She leaned in close to Anya's face. "And most of all...." She kissed her softly on the lips. "Believe."

The woman and the soft glow surrounding her

faded quickly, and Anya placed her fingertips to her lips. *What just happened?*

"Aine?" he called again.

"I'm coming." If she was in Ireland of the past, she didn't want to be out in the dark alone.

***

Anya stood close to the fire, warming her hands and thinking about the strange young woman. Had Carrick seen her?

"As soon as I finish the last of the herbs, we will eat," he said.

"Thank you."

"It will only be a moment."

He bent to grab a handful of St. John's Wort flowers from the basket, his trim backside filling out his trousers. She blushed. It had been a long time since she had so thoroughly examined a man's finer features, and the warmth that filled her flooded her senses. He tossed the flowers into the fire, and the flames danced up then retreated.

"What are those plants for?"

"They keep away evil spirits. Same with these herbs." He took sprigs of green from a pack and added them to the fire. Deep earthy smells rose and enveloped the air surrounding them.

She inhaled deeply. The woodsy scent reminded her of dark forests and damp mushrooms.

"Solstice eve is a prime time for evil spirits to do their magic."

He wiped his brow. "It's very warm." He shed his tunic and Anya gawked.

"Are you disturbed?"

She shook her head. Faint perspiration glistened on his chest like the moonlight on the stones, his abs just as hard and chiseled. He noticed her stare and smiled.

She looked away, sure he noticed her blush.

"Just a couple more logs and then we eat."

His voice lilted with what must have been a broad smile. She'd been caught with her hand in the cookie jar. And apparently, he liked it.

She sat cross-legged on the pile of blankets beside him, his long legs stretched out. He opened the food basket, pulled out a round loaf of dark bread and a chunk of cheese. In the moonlight, the dinner rivaled the finest candlelit dinner in Paris. Her heart thudded as he leaned near.

"We'll share the mead," he said. He took a long drink then held the vessel to her lips and tipped it. She drank, gulping the warm, yeasty beverage. After a few mouthfuls, she pushed it away and wiped her mouth with the back of her hand.

"Thank you." Tasting like warm earth and sunshine, it wasn't like any beer she'd ever had.

Tipping up the mead, he swallowed, his neck muscles working. Her cheeks burned. He set the vessel down and grinned at her. "It is good?"

"Very," she murmured.

He tore a piece of bread from the loaf and handed it to her. "I think I have some butter here in the basket. Would you like some?"

"That would be lovely." He dug in the basket, his dark hair falling forward and concealing his face.

"Here it is! The best in my village—from the best cows in our area."

She handed the crusty bread to him, and he spread a layer of creamy butter over it.

"Thank you."

"Let me help," he said. "Just taste. Don't think about anything else. Only taste."

She hesitated, then closed her eyes and opened her mouth a bit, aware of his stare.

"Wider."

The hard crust slipped between her lips, the butter melting as soon as it touched her tongue. She groaned and savored the bite of bread.

"Good?" He laughed.

A gorgeous man without a shirt was feeding her. *Very good...*"Yes."

He wiped her lower lip with his thumb.

"I am glad you like it." He handed her the rest of the piece.

"Thank you."

He tore off another chunk and took a bite. "We have a decent life here, when there is no war."

"Is there often fighting? It looks so peaceful." She licked the last traces of butter from her lips.

His scowled. "Almost always. The kings rise and drop as frequently as the crops. Blood falls like rain."

She hesitated, unsure how much to ask. "But you're not a soldier?"

He broke off a piece of cheese and handed it to her. "No. I do not fight. I am a druid. I train to heal, to see, to move through time. One day soon, I will be a full Ovate. Kings will honor me. Until I displease one of them, then my blood will join the others." He popped a chunk into his mouth.

"What about your family?" Ireland of the past was barbaric and scary. History was dark about many things, except the violence and turmoil of the time. She stretched her legs. A lone owl hooted from the trees beyond the stones and the breeze blew colder. Carrick didn't seem fazed by the weather, or the darkness. He looked like a warrior, even if he was only a troubled soul.

He gazed directly into her eyes. "I have no family anymore."

She lost herself in the depth of his stare, and for a second, she didn't feel lonely. "Nor do I," she whispered. He looked away and tore off another piece of the loaf.

He studied the bread. The creamy butter would melt if he didn't eat it quickly, but he didn't want to look at Anya yet. The woman, or fay, had walked into the stone circle and gotten too close, and quickly. She was supposed to be a physical release, and *oh yes*, he wanted that, but he also wanted to console her and make her feel safe. What had happened to his resolve? And how would his caretaking affect his Ovate initiation?

She stared off across the circle, and he memorized her profile. Her milky white skin, the high forehead and short, upturned nose sitting above full lips—she was beautiful. She glanced his way, her blue eyes wide and not-quite innocent, but naïve.

"You are lonely?" He stuffed the bread in his mouth.

She faced the fire again. "Does it matter? Aren't we all fated to be lonely?"

"It seems that is our destiny," he mumbled. "Would you like some more mead?"

"Yes, please." She tipped the vessel and drank. Wind gusted through the circle, and he reached to push her hair away from her face. He stopped, then ran his finger over her soft cheek.

"I can't believe one so lovely is lonely."

She ducked her head again. "I am bound by my job and responsibilities. I have no family. My life hasn't followed the normal path."

"Mine has been the same. My duties have kept me from many worldly things. A druid life—especially the Ovate druid—is solitary."

"I see." She nodded. "The fire is getting low. Perhaps you should tend it."

"Indeed. Come with me, and then let's walk around the circle, and I will tell you about the Grange and druids and you can tell me about your job."

"Okay."

He brushed the crumbs off his pants and slipped his shirt back on. The night air had begun to cool the valley, and he searched the sky for the crescent moon. Still hours until sunrise. It would come too soon. Would he hold her in his arms before the sun appeared?

Slipping his hand in hers, he led her to the fire. The hearth radiated warmth, and the glow lit her face. She smiled, though her path was marked with sadness, too.

He gave her a handful of star flowers. "Toss these."

She flung the flowers into the air and they floated down into the inferno, blazing and popping in tiny sparkles. He took her into his arms without thinking, hugged her close. She lay her head on his chest.

"Let's take that walk."

"Slip off your shoes so you can feel the grass."

"Okay, but you have to, too."

He set her sandals and his boots near his pallet. Was he making the right choice, tempting the fates to risk getting closer to Aine?

As they walked around the interior edge of the circle, hand-in-hand, he told her about the ancient people who had set the stones. One hundred thirteen stones in all, all upright and standing shoulder to shoulder in a wide circle. Many festivals and events had been held there under both the moon and stars, and the circle was truly sacred, brimming with the enchantment of thousands of years.

"If you stand really still, you can feel the magic coming up through your feet."

"I feel it," she said. "The vibration."

"The magic is powerful here. And old. Every time I touch these stones, I feel the hands of a thousand people in the same place, seeking knowledge, seeking answers, seeking love."

She touched each bump and ridge on a large stone, feeling the surface tenderly, like it was a lover. He gulped.

"Let me show you the entrance."

"Where I came in?"

"Yes, but there is something very special that I should tell you about those two boulders. I think you will find the story quite amazing."

He led her to two of the largest stones in the circle. Unlike the other rocks, they were separated, with a space between them large enough to pass through. Moss grew heavy on one side and the grass between them lay flattened.

"Magnificent," she said. "I have never traveled to Ireland, but I will have to do so now."

"These rocks have a purpose, other than to provide an entrance." He stood spread eagle in the entrance. "On the sunrise of solstice in the summer, the sun rises between these stones and shines straight across the circle in a long golden line."

"Oh! That must be glorious."

"It is the most magical sunrise of the year here at the Grange. And it's tomorrow morning."

"Oh my! I can't wait to see it! Is that why you're here? In preparation?"

"Yes, I must tend the solstice fire the entire night until the sun breaks through the pathway."

She covered her mouth and jumped up and down. He laughed. It was good to see her happy like a child.

She hugged him. When he moved her gently back against the cool stone, she didn't resist. The fabric of her dress was so soft, it must be fay-made, or truly she wasn't of his world.

"Tell me the truth, Aine," he said. "Are you fay?" He rested his hands on the stone above her, and pressed against her. She closed her eyes.

"No, I'm not. I was brought here by Eve, to your time. To be with you. But I am not fay."

The vision before him was more than he could take. He drew her into a kiss. When her tongue met his, heat surged through him at her boldness, and he pulled her deeper.

She rubbed his back, then grabbed his ass and pressed closer. He pushed back, hard. Gasping for breath, she moved away from his kiss.

She giggled. He pushed her back against the stone, and they both fought for control of the kiss until he thought he would explode from desire to possess her. She collapsed against the stone as he kissed her cheeks, then her neck, nipping and sucking as he held her up. Oh, the night was not long enough to do the things he wanted to do.

He leaned away and looked at her, her full lips swollen from his onslaught, her eyes glazed over with passion. How he ached to lay her down on the cool grass and take her right then.

"Why are you stopping?" she asked.

"The fire." He arranged his stiff cock in his pants. "I have to tend it."

"But my fire burns, too."

He ground against her, caressing her breast. "I am not done with you."

"I'll wait on the blankets," she said. "Hurry."

Anya sat on the blanket as Carrick tossed wood on the solstice blaze. The damned ritual. She'd never been set aside for a campfire, of all things—and by a boy scout druid. Hopefully, he'd put enough wood on it to make it last long enough. For what? Long enough for a roll in the grass? Outside? In Ireland? The night had gotten twisted, but strangely, it felt right. It would be okay.

She sighed. Every nerve ached and she needed release. She cupped her pussy through her dress. *Hurry up.*

Finally, he headed toward her. She brushed aside the errant bread crumbs and sat up on her knees.

He smiled. The time away had not altered his mood. His pants bulged.

"Come here." she said.

His muscles flexed as he stripped off his shirt. She stroked his abs, tracing the faint line of soft dark hair below his belly button. He flinched and the bulge in his pants grew harder. He doubled over as she leaned forward and nuzzled him.

She undid the knot on his pants and slid them down. His cock bobbed and she stroked it softly. He moaned and dropped to his knees.

He drew her to him and kissed her.

"Is this what you want? Say so now, before I am unable to stop."

"Oh, yes," she said. "I want you. Now."

He lifted her dress over her head, tossing it into a heap beside them. The night breeze touched her skin and she shivered. Carrick traced her shoulder with a fingertip then down her arm and back up, stopping at her bra strap.

"What is this?"

"A bra," she giggled. "I'll take it off." She popped the clasp. Her breasts bounced free in the cool night air, her nipples tightening. In a flash, he was on her, sucking and nipping at her breasts. She lay back on the blankets, hoping he would focus on one nipple long enough to give her pleasure, but he was intent on being everywhere at once.

His cock pressed against her. He stopped and gazed at her, his eyes hooded with lust. He grasped the crotch of her panties and tugged them down and off with a single motion, almost tearing them away. He obviously knew what underwear was. Licking then kissing her stomach, he inched lower to her shaved pussy and slid a finger in before slipping his tongue in beside it.

"Oh, Carrick." She moaned. He pushed deeper while he lapped and teased. She writhed against him, forgetting her job, her loneliness, being in Ireland. His movements sped and pressure and warmth spread, growing and burning.

"Yes." The heat built and finally exploded like starflowers popping the solstice fire. He moved up to lie beside her.

She shuddered—more from pleasure than cold. And a little from embarrassment. It had been a long time since she opened up like that to a guy. Still, his warm tongue made it pretty easy. Grasping his cock, she stroked. He groaned and rubbed against her leg. Oh yes, he still wanted her.

Her purse lay just beyond reach and she moved to retrieve it.

"What are you doing?" He stroked himself lightly. "We still have time before dawn."

"Oh, we're just getting started."

She felt for the foil packet from the side zipper. The condoms had been there for ages, and she hoped they hadn't expired or gotten dry. Still, she always believed in being prepared, even if the odds were not in her favor for using them.

"What is that?"

"Just a little covering to protect us. Trust me." She leaned over and rolled the condom onto him.

Before he could ask another question, she kissed him and forced him back onto the blanket. She lay full length on top of him, his hard body firm and hot under her soft one. She eased her legs open and sat astride him.

She watched him. The moonlight spread blue across his pale face and his dark hair splayed out onto the blanket. He needed release. She lifted off him enough to position his cock. He opened his mouth to speak, but she eased onto him before he could. He grabbed her hips and moaned.

She loved his length filling her. As she moved, he held on tightly, trying to lift into her.

"Wait," she whispered. "It's my turn to pleasure you."

"Please. I cannot wait."

He pulled her down harder and harder. She rode him, wanting each stroke to last a little longer, go a little deeper. Closing her eyes, she savored the cool night air and the heat between her legs.

"Enough," he said.

She opened her mouth to protest, but in a quick motion, he flipped her onto her back. "I need to...."

"Yes." She opened her knees.

He thrust into her, and she rose to meet him. The night stilled around them, the only sounds flesh on flesh and puffs of breath. He groaned and her own climax rushed in, smaller, but satisfying. She rolled over and into his arms. He hugged her close and kissed the top of her head.

***

Carrick lay still, breathing in the night air. Solstice eve had not unfolded as he had planned. What had promised to be a night of quiet introspection had become an evening he would long remember—for different reasons. Aine slept against his shoulder, her hair trailing across his bare chest like a soft blanket.

She stirred, rubbed her nose then drifted back into sleep. He ran his hand over her head and down her hair, her cheek warm against his chest. Overhead, a star trailed long and winked out. A good omen. This night was magically blessed. *I don't need the stars to tell me how fortunate I am.*

He gently slipped from under her. She moaned and he fought the urge to take her in his arms again. He covered her with one of the blankets. To feel her one more time before morning would be bliss. But right now, the fire.

The landscape beyond the stones was completely invisible, covered in the dense mist that rose from the loch. Had the fay watched their lovemaking? He stretched as the cool air circled his bare skin. *I hope they are jealous.* The night lay silent, no sounds reaching up from the loch. Even the insects slept. In the darkest hours of night just before dawn, man made his decisions and chose his path. He grabbed his trousers and tunic.

The stone hearth's heat warmed his feet. He stared into the embers for a moment. Did he want to spend his life alone? The woodpile had grown small overnight, and day would break too soon. Already the sky lay heavy with expectancy. Danu would come to retrieve Aine, and all would go back to normal. Alone again.

He sat beside her. She rolled over toward him, still sleeping, her hair a hazy nest around her head. He smiled and adjusted the blanket over her bare shoulder. It had been a long time, nigh forever, since he had found such peace with a woman.

He swirled the mead in the jar. Mostly gone. He drank a long drink then set it down and gazed out over the grassy circle. Silence lay as heavy as the mist. To the east, the sky prepared to burst into dawn.

Faint streaks of orange lay low on the horizon and wisps of clouds, vibrant pink and purple, swirled low. An eagle streaked over the circle, hunting rabbits venturing from their warrens. The world was coming alive again, and the fay would soon release their hold on the circle. He had to wake her before their time was over.

"Aine?" He shook her gently.

She rolled onto her back, eyes closed. Brushing the hair out of her face, he bent down and put his lips to hers. She murmured then wrapped her arms around his neck. Dizzy with need, he sank into her wet kiss.

She yawned. "Is it morning?"

"Almost," he whispered. "Look toward the entry stones. You can see the sky beginning to lighten." He handed the sundress to her.

"I want to see the sun rise. Can we take a blanket over to the stones?"

"Yes." He stood and sipped from the waterskin. "Do you want some water? The mead is gone."

She slipped the dress over her head and the pale blue fabric fluttered over her. "Yes, thank you." She reached for the water then grabbed another foil packet.

He grinned. "We are going to celebrate the sun rise? Protected?"

She ducked her head and her hair fell forward. He pulled her to him and lifted her chin so her eyes met his. "Do not be embarrassed." He kissed her softly on the lips, each eyelid then on her forehead. "Let us go before the sun makes its appearance."

He picked up several blankets and they headed toward the entry stones. The sky lightened with purples and pinks and the trees stood in dark silhouette against the lightening sky. Too soon. The sun was coming too soon.

"Today will be the longest day of the year." She bent to pluck a white daisy from the grass. She twirled it between her fingertips before sticking it in her hair. "I love summer."

"It will be the longest day in my lifetime. You will be gone."

She wrapped her arm through his, and they walked in silence to the opening of the circle. The pang of separation already stung.

"Here?" He pointed to an area near the edge of the stone circle.

"Just inside the entry stones. I want to see the sun as it rises."

He spread the blankets out on the grass. She tossed the packet down and sat cross-legged, patting the blanket beside her.

"Come on," she said. "Sit down."

He sat until her body molded against his arm and hip. "You didn't tell me about your job," he said. "The one that keeps you from being happy."

"I don't want to ruin this morning. Let's just say I am devoted to a lost cause. I won't be going back to it."

More pinks painted the sky, and birds awoke and sang their morning songs. The low sounds of cows carried over the meadows. Day was imminent.

"Look! The mist is almost gone."

"The fay sweep the mist away as they retire in the morning."

She lay down, putting her head in his lap and his cock stirred. He stroked her hair and watched the rise and fall of her breasts beneath the thin fabric. How much longer could he wait to move inside her again? Was it already too late?

Anya relaxed, aware of the hardness in Carrick's

trousers. He rubbed against her back. The sky had begun to fill with the pinks and oranges of dawn. The sun would rise soon and the night would officially be over. The best night of her life was about to end. Then it would be back to pubs on a Saturday night. At least she'd made a decision not to go back to working for old man Mitchell. Time was on her side for the moment, and she could be with the man of her dreams in the last minutes before the sun fully rose.

She rolled over so that her face was in Carrick's lap. She began planting firm kisses on his thighs, up and down then between his legs and over the hardness there. He pressed her head closer. His passion fueled her to work more quickly, and she ran her hands up his legs to his cock, squeezing it through his pants.

He moaned. "Aine."

"Take off your shirt," she whispered.

He ripped the tunic over his head and tossed it to the side then started to pull his trousers down, but she stopped him.

"I'll take care of those."

She ran her hand along the tied waistband where cloth met skin, then followed with her tongue, tracing the path again and again. His skin tasted warm and earthy like the mead, and all man.

She traced the line of dark hair trailing down into his pants. He jerked when she slipped the tip of her tongue under the waistband, touching the tip of his cock with her wet mouth.

His musky scent drove her to explore deeper, and she edged his pants down, freeing his cock. The world was waking around her and she had to hurry. She licked her lips in anticipation. He shuddered when she lowered her head to take him between her lips.

As she sucked, she wished the moment could last

forever. She savored his salty taste, the velvety softness of his skin, and his pulsing warmth. She took him again and again, stroking and licking. Living in the moment. He moaned and thrust into her mouth, and she wanted nothing more in the world than to bring him pleasure.

"Stop!" He quivered.

"What's wrong?" Numb from the friction on her lips, the words tumbled out awkwardly.

"The sun is rising." He searched the blanket. "I think we need this?" He tore open the package and slipped the condom on.

She laughed.

"First, lie back so I can look at you."

"But..."

"Lie back. I want to remember everything about you." He nudged her shoulders gently. "Now open your legs and lift your dress."

The first rays of the sun were streaking through the stones, casting long shadows and golden highlights across the circle. His face was couched in shadow, but his eyes were half-closed with desire.

She hesitated then tugged her dress to her waist, the sunlight warming her skin. Carrick's sharp intake of breath told her he was pleased with what he saw. He covered her body with his, shoving her dress up above her breasts and thrusting into her with one motion.

"Look at me," he grunted. "I want to see your pleasure."

His face was bathed in golden sunlight, and his blue eyes sparkled. He thrust again. She wrapped her legs around his waist.

"I don't want this to end."

"Me, either." Shocks of pleasure grew and spiraled through her.

He gazed into her eyes, seeing through the

loneliness and into her soul. As the sunlight warmed the air, he began a rhythm that brought them both to the brink. Her climax overtook her, and she tried not to close her eyes. He pushed deep and stilled. A low groan signaled his release and he collapsed. She hugged him tightly. Dawn had arrived and the circle could be filled with druids or villagers at any moment, but she didn't want to move. The stillness was perfect.

"Why are you so quiet?" she asked.

"I am unhappy that our time is near over."

She nodded. Damn short night. Figured she would have a date on the shortest night of the year.

He pointed. "Look!"

The sun was midway through the entry stones, its rays streaming golden and warm and lighting up an arc of the circle.

"It's beautiful," she breathed.

He clasped her hand. "I'll not forget this night. The sunrise will always remind me of you."

A sob caught in her throat. If the night had not been so perfect, the sentiment would have been really lame.

A dark shadow crept over the strip of sunlight. What was it?

"Aine?" the voice said. "Carrick?"

"What do you want?" Their time couldn't end. It wasn't fair. She'd finally found someone she could share with. Why did he have to be from another century?

"The night is over."

"Danu. You are back for Aine." Carrick stood and helped Anya to her feet.

"Yes." The fay moved into the grassy circle. "The night is over and now it is time for Aine to go home."

"No! I don't want to leave!" She covered her mouth as soon as she said it. Her face flushed. What if he didn't want her to stay? *I really knew how to make a fool of myself. I could ruin anything, given the chance.*

Danu glided to them and placed her fingertips on Anya's cheeks. "Do you remember what I said?"

She swore she heard water trickling. Or was it Danu's voice? *Trust. Believe.* She looked at the fairy and nodded.

"Then you know what to do."

"Will it work?"

"That is up to you both." Danu shimmered in the early light. "But time is short."

Anya kissed Danu on the cheek and turned to Carrick. *I can do it.* It wasn't about being impulsive or a risk-taker. It was about living life to the fullest. Grabbing opportunity. Believing in yourself. She took a deep breath.

"Will you come with me? To my time?"

"Is it possible?" Danu gave a slight nod. He pulled Anya close. "Of course, I will! There is nothing for me here but sadness and stagnation. You have shown me true energy and magic. I feel life beginning anew."

"The mead isn't as good in my time."

"We'll make do. As long as we are together."

She smiled at Danu. The fairy winked back.

"Are you certain this is what you want?"

"I've never been more sure of anything."

"Then close your eyes and kiss me," Anya said. "Anything is possible. You just have to believe." Light mist swirled around them.

"I'm ready."

As his lips met hers, the light mist became a splashing fountain and the cool Irish morning became a late summer evening in a little mountain town.

Pharoah, Mine

Book 3

Dedication

To Ophelia and Giselle...

Pharoah, Mine

Kathryn Adams is a veterinarian with a cause—she risks her financial security to help local cat rescue groups. When a stray cat, black with one green eye and one blue, meows at her door one night, Kathryn's view of rescues changes quickly.

In Ancient Egypt, the throne is passed to the firstborn son, and when the sun rises over his father's fresh tomb, Seti will claim his crown. He doesn't want to rule, but the only other option is death, and his half-brother is happy to oblige.

Seti and Kathryn each need fulfillment in their lives. Through the help of Madame Eve and an ancient Egyptian goddess, they find peace in each other's arms for one night. At dawn, Bast will return to ferry them back to their responsibilities unless they can rescue each other.

Chapter One

"He came through surgery just fine. Such a sweet little guy."

"Thank you so much. I was worried about him."

"Routine. He did great."

"Are you sure he's able to go home already?"

Dr. Katharine Adams peered into the tiny blue carrier. The ball of gray fluff peeped at her then rested his head on his paws. Soft purring resonated in the cage. *So cute.* "He's fine. I've given him an injection of pain medication that will last until tomorrow. Keep him in a quiet place tonight and follow the post-op instructions my tech went over with you. She'll be on call all weekend if you have any questions or concerns."

"Call me any time," Missy said, smiling.

"Thanks, again. You do good work here." The woman picked the carrier up off the counter and peeked at the tiny kitten.

Missy held the door open for her then locked it behind her, keys jangling. "Long day. I'm beat."

Katharine pulled her nametag off and tossed it on the counter. "Me, too. No surgeries tomorrow, but the Paws4U group is bringing in ten cats for Monday's schedule."

"That is a lot in one day."

"Yeah, but I have to do them. I can't let the rescue groups down."

"I'm going to hang out here in the morning while on call, so I'll intake them. Take a day off." Missy flipped the small reception room's lights off. "Grab some dinner?" She headed for the back rooms.

"Not unless you're up for reheat. I've got paperwork." She followed, yawning. "And I'll sleep here tonight. I'll help you intake in the morning."

"Listen." Missy stopped in the hallway, and Katharine nearly bumped into her. "You've got to take a break. You can't keep this up."

"I have to keep working. I can't afford more than two vet techs and a receptionist."

"You don't have to do all those low-cost spay and neuters for the rescues." Her friend folded her arms. "You'd make a lot more money if you didn't."

Katharine pushed by her into the break room. "You know it isn't about the money. I can't bear knowing that so many animals are euthanized needlessly. I do what I can." She yanked the refrigerator door open and scanned the leftovers. Stew. Kung Pao chicken. Veggie wrap. This job was more than a paycheck. *Dammit.*

"Katharine."

She moved the Kung Pao chicken aside and grabbed the veggie wrap and a bottle of water. Missy touched her arm.

"What?" The irritability in her own voice surprised her.

"I know saving cats means everything to you. All I'm saying is maybe you're working too much. Maybe you need to do less. Or find another veterinarian to share the responsibilities. That's all."

Her shoulders slumped. She set her food on the small wooden table. "It's hard to cut back when I know so many animals are in need. With all the expenditures, the clinic is already in the red, and I can't take on any more debt."

"You have to take care of yourself, too." Missy grabbed a bottled water from the fridge. "I've been thinking a lot about this."

"About what? Not much I can do until the clinic starts making more money."

"About you and your sacrifices, and the fact you have zero personal life. I think you need a love life."

Katharine laughed and plopped down in the chair. The cold veggie wrap stuck to the paper as she peeled it away, and she picked at the soft bread, annoyed. "That is hilarious! And, assuming I actually had someone to go out with, *when* would I find time to go on said date? I can barely find time to clean my townhouse." She took a bite of her food. *A date, ha*!

Missy smirked. "How long have we known each other?"

"Um. I assume that's rhetorical. But for fun, well, since my last year of school. So, about six years."

"And when's the last time you had a boyfriend?" She slammed her water bottle on the table.

"Well, I had coffee with that researcher from Cornell last fall...."

"That wasn't a date, and he wasn't a boyfriend. He wanted a donation."

"Um, well, I guess it would be Bill, then. You remember, the college jerk. Mr. Wrong in all the right ways." Stuffing another bite into her mouth, Katharine mumbled, "Does he count?"

Missy groaned. "Seriously?"

"*Seriously* does he count? Or *seriously* is he the last guy I dated?" Katharine smiled. *Got her*.

"You're impossible!"

"Thanks. I try." She popped the last of the wrap into her mouth and balled up the paper.

"Hold on. You aren't leaving yet. I have a surprise for you."

"Unless you've found more time you can give me...."

"I was going to tell you at dinner—but since you

decided to wolf down a five minute meal here at the clinic, I guess I'll have to tell you now. Kind of appropriate, given the circumstances."

"It's not my birthday." Missy was uptight. Nervous. *What's up with her*? "Spill!"

"Well, like I said, I've been thinking you need a date...."

"And you have a cousin in town?"

She laughed. "No, no, it isn't that simple."

Katharine's hands went cold. *No way.* "I'm not going on a blind date."

"Before you say no, listen to me a minute—"

"No way. Absolutely not." She yanked the ponytail holder out of her hair and shook the long strands loose. "Now, I am going to get out of my scrubs and shower. I have paperwork to do."

"Listen to me. This isn't what you're thinking. You're lonely. It's one night together, that's all." Missy grinned. "And I've already set it up."

"You got me a prostitute? Is this some kind of joke?" Her heart fluttered, as adrenaline poured through her.

"No. It's Madame Eve's 1Night Stand. My sister's friend used the service after her divorce. Found her soul mate."

Katharine blinked and watched her for any sign she was joking. Missy stared back at her, swirling her water bottle.

"Anyway, they faxed over a receipt and some more information. I put the papers on your desk. Speaking of food, I've got to go—I'm starving and I need to be back here early. Have fun! And read the fax."

"You're crazy. Certifiable."

"And you're a veterinarian, not a psychiatrist. Think about it, okay? No commitment. Consider it."

"I appreciate your concern, but there's no way in

hell I'm having a one-night stand."

"Get your paperwork done. And please don't let me come in here tomorrow morning and find you still here."

Chapter Two

The king's sarcophagus lay on a large carved stone in the center of the torch-lit chamber. Seti paced across the compacted dirt, the oily smoke from the flames trailing behind him in a whirlwind of memory. Musky incense swirled over mounds of beaded offerings to the gods. He fell onto his knees, trembling. The lone melody of a cane ney flute snaked down into the tomb, the musician somewhere outside, with most of the mourners.

"Father," he whispered. No tears came. He fingered the painted hieroglyphs lining the edges of the wooden likeness of his sire. The markings told stories of the king's honored past. The wars. The blood. The lives cut short and the many children. *Many brothers.*

"And I am firstborn. Why?" He pressed his sandaled toe against the earthen floor and balled his hands into fists. Shaking, he stormed over to the servants who knelt by the vizier at the tomb's entrance. "Leave!"

The servants, half-bowing, scampered through the low doorway. Seti shook his head. They scurried like startled rats.

"My king, you must calm down," the vizier said. The old man moved his staff side to side, in deference.

"I am not yet king, Pensekhmet. Not until morning." Seti rested his head on his father's image, freshly kohled on the surface of the painted wooden coffin. The pigments smelled of sharp pine and heavy clay, alive and fresh, but his bitter old father lay inside—wrapped in linen and empty of his soul. The tyrant had finally passed into the afterworld. Even now, he walked with the gods.

"When the sun rises, you will be king. It is time to put away your childish notions and accept your destiny."

Seti beat his fists against the wood in a slow rhythm. "I do not want to rule Egypt."

"You are foolish and young. You will rule."

"I do not want to marry Sebi."

"You can have as many wives as you wish, once you are king. But your sister must bear your heir."

"I don't want many wives. I want happiness. Even in this sacred place of my ancestors, I know something else awaits me out there. Someone. I feel it in my very bones."

The vizier grasped his shoulder with a crinkled hand and squeezed. "My king, you are suffering. Your father has died, and you need respite. It is understandable. You don't mean what you say."

Seti lifted his face and blurs of paint smudged his father's image. He would not cry or bemoan fate. An answer would come.

"I will find your mother. She is worried about you." The vizier had aged much since his appointment and he leaned on his staff.

Kindness softened Seti's tone. "Are you happy, Pensekhmet?"

"I am not happy at your father's passing."

"No, I mean really happy. Does your heart fill to bursting each morning when you greet the sun?"

Pensekhmet laughed. "I don't think anyone is that happy, but I won't complain. I've had a good life."

"Then you are fulfilled?"

"As much as I expect to be. But you are young and abundant rewards await you. You will find your path—and you'll have all of Egypt at your feet."

Seti gazed around the tomb, the hazy halo of oily torchlight casting a pall over the vault.

"Your mother is waiting to come in to look upon your father's sarcophagus for the last time," Pensekhmet said. "I will tell her you wish to talk."

"Thank you."

The vizier straightened. "When you are done, the boat is prepared for your journey. The Nile is peaceful tonight under the glorious, deep moon, and it won't take you long to reach the royal home we've prepared for you. You can celebrate your impending coronation."

"As you wish. But I want to be alone."

"But it's customary—"

"I don't care. You may send servants in the morning. I'll return to the city in the grand parade as you wish. But tonight, I'll sleep alone."

"You must have guards," the vizier said. "Your brother may do something foolish."

"They are to stay outside the compound."

"As you require." The vizier bent to go through the small doorway.

Seti sighed. The large sarcophagus, probably five times bigger than his father, dominated the small room. Much as he had when alive. Canopic jars, carved jewelry, and baskets of dried fruit covered the perimeter of the tomb. Offerings made to facilitate the king's journey to the afterworld. *Pray the gods can handle him.*

At sunrise, the tomb opening would be sealed for eternity and his own reign would begin. With a grand procession into the city, he'd claim his place among the great kings of Egypt. *I don't want to build temples. I don't want to send men to war. I'm not like my father.*

A large cat, painted in abundant detail, peered down at him. Bastet. His favorite goddess. Not the most powerful goddess, but revered, nonetheless. His own palace would be filled with cats, wearing necklaces of gold. He laughed, imagining the hallways teeming with royal felines. Only one had shared his father's table.

"Father, you would not approve."

"I think it's marvelous," a voice purred.

"What?"

"I said, I think lots of cats in the palace is a marvelous idea." A warm, slinky tail wrapped around his leg then disappeared.

"Surely, my emotions have overtaken me."

At the entrance of the tomb stood a woman dressed in a long gown, wearing a jeweled collar. Her eyes, one blue and one green, sparkled in the torchlight like the gems on the offering tables.

"Bastet?" Cold swept through him, and the hairs on his neck stood.

"Yes." She slunk toward him. "You do not want to rule this empire, Seti? Why not?"

"I-I-I am not the warring kind. I want to heal, not kill. Ruling is not in my blood."

"Oh, but the gods say it is in your blood. You are of divine birth." She slipped an arm around his neck and nuzzled close.

The press of her breasts in the soft fabric against his bare chest should have given him pleasure, but he shook with fear. *I've angered the gods.* "What do you want, Goddess?"

"You do deserve love, my dear Seti. Can you trust me?"

"Of course I trust the direction of the gods. What will you have of me?"

"Eve will help you. But you must willingly accept.

Only then will you be fulfilled."

"My coronation is tomorrow. How will this eve help me—nothing can stop the dawn."

She stroked his back, and a deep vibration in her chest rolled up and expanded throughout her. Her eyes glowed. "Trust me, trust Madame Eve—she will help you. Someone will come. This person will also have needs. You will help her and perhaps you will find what you seek."

"I don't know...."

"She won't be from this time, or this Egypt."

"I don't understand."

"She will appear foreign to you, but know this: she will bring you joy. Trust Eve."

"From where will she come?"

Her nose twitched. "I am not certain yet. But you only have tonight, so hurry and make your decision. One night could change your path."

"But...." He tensed.

She licked his cheek and vanished.

Chapter Three

Katharine combed out her wet hair in long strokes. A shower, even at the clinic, always relaxed her. After pulling on her favorite worn jeans and black tank top, she slipped on the sandals from her bag of spare clothing. *Thank goodness I don't have much paperwork.* She yawned. Sleeping on the pullout sofa in her office would be a lot easier than driving home. *Maybe I won't even pull it out.*

As the coffeemaker hissed and steamed, she searched for her favorite cup among the mismatched dishes piled in the drainer. Two spoons of sugar, stir, and instant alertness. At least for half an hour or so. She opened the outer door to the small back porch off her office. The coffee smelled of nutty chocolate and warmed her from the inside.

The night spread in front of her, with early fall slipping leaves down from trees like whispers. The crickets of summer had quieted and the night lay almost still. The rocking chair creaked as she rocked, cutting into the silence. A chill ran up her back. Not many more nights left to sit outside wearing a tank top. She blew across the top of the coffee and watched the steam whisk away on her breath.

The fax from Madame Eve proved interesting, albeit a little nerve wracking. The promise of a secret night intrigued her. She'd read books with plenty of stories of one-night stands going well—even leading to marriage. But participating in one? She gulped her coffee. In the distance, two lights blinked in the sky—

blue and green, like tiny beacons.

Do people really do this? Missy said she knew someone who had. Closing her eyes, she concentrated on the creak of the chair and the low rustle of leaves. The coffee cup warming her hands, she leaned back and closed her eyes.

She blinked awake, shivering, the cup cold. *A one-night stand would be more fun than paperwork. What would be the harm?*

Heading inside, she saw the clock read nine p.m. *That's it? Feels much later.* She set the mug on her desk. "Missy is right; all I do is work. How did my life get to the point of just work, work, work? I used to go out and have fun. Screw it. The paperwork can wait."

She grabbed the blanket and pillow from the storage ottoman and tossed them on the couch, not bothering to pull it out.

Pulling the blanket up, she settled on the couch. How bad could the date be? *I could at least meet the guy.* Besides, the fax said Madame Eve really tried to match people's interests. Couldn't be any worse than some of the guys she'd picked.

Her eyelids drooped and closed. She had to find a way to make more money at the clinic without charging the rescues. *How can I balance my life when my checkbook is in such disarray?*

The rap, rap, rap was quiet but persistent—like a branch tapping out a cadence on a glass pane. She sat up slowly. Midnight.

The blanket slid to the floor as she stood. The rapping continued, and she crept over to the door and paused. It could only be an emergency at this hour. "Who is it?" No answer.

The knocking stopped. "Meow."

It wasn't the kitten "meow" of a tiny baby or the painful "meow" of an injured animal, but a confident "meow." Puzzled, she opened the door. A black cat slunk into the office, swirling around her legs once then hopping onto the couch.

"Meow?"

She closed and locked the door.

"Well, what are you doing here?" She stroked the animal. Its eyes sparkled—one blue and one green—appearing to smile at her with upturned whiskers. "Who do you belong to?"

She scratched its neck and discovered a single strand of golden chain set with a green stone. "Interesting. But no contact information."

The cat purred and rubbed its head against her. "You are so beautiful. You must belong to someone. What are you doing here?"

"Meow?"

Katharine sighed. Why did people let their animals roam free? Out here, near the woods, a coyote could easily take a small animal. "Well, if you are staying with me tonight, let me close my office door so you can't wander. I'd better get you a box and food and water, too."

She arranged the supplies in the corner. It wasn't the first time a stray had made a home in her office, but Missy would be tsk tsking when she found out. Stray animals should go in the quarantine kennel.

"Have you even moved?"

"Meow?" The cat washed.

"I've got to sleep. You need to scoot over."

She crawled back onto the couch and covered up. It curled up on her chest, eyes closed, purring.

"Bastet."

"Whaa?" Katharine mumbled. She tried to roll over, but the cat didn't move.

"I am Bastet," it said.

"And I am dreaming."

"Not a dream. I am real."

"I need sleep."

"No, Madame Eve sent me to deliver you to your date. We must go now." The cat's eyes gleamed in the moonlit room.

"Huh?" She struggled to sit, but the animal seemed to gain weight and pin her down.

"Relax, Katharine." It peered at her, but its mouth didn't move as the words were spoken. "I am Bastet. I'll protect you. You have to trust me."

"Crazy cat—or crazy me, rather—what a weird dream." She pretended to sleep. When she peeked, the animal's eyes were glowing green and blue, and she sank deeper into the couch. She fell, head over feet, screaming silently.

Chapter Four

Seti stepped out of the tomb and into the fresh air. The guards bowed to him as he glanced at his father's open burial house for the last time. Tomorrow, it would be forever sealed. *Thankfully.*

Fires burned in sand pits all around the ceremonial circle—keeping evil spirits away from his ancestors while the tomb lay open. His father may have been a bad king, but he was still king of Egypt— the greatest land known. *How many are celebrating his death? How many look to me to rule?* The ney music stopped. *How many wish my brother would ascend the throne instead of me?*

"Seti!"

His mother rushed to him. Her white mourning sheath was covered in long strands of beads that clinked as she jogged toward him. Though she smiled, he knew it wasn't sincere.

"Mother. It's good to see you." He held his hands out to her.

"Is it?" She raised a kohled eyebrow. Her sleek black hair fell to her shoulders then stopped in a harsh line, as if it dared not disobey. Few things disobeyed his mother.

"Always." He kissed her forehead.

"Let's walk. I must talk to you."

"I am traveling up the Nile to the country home tonight. I don't have long." He folded his arms over his chest. The warm breeze refreshed him, after the stifling heat of the tomb.

"Yes, tradition. Pensekhmet said you wish to be alone tonight. No women?"

"I am tired." He gazed out over the dark horizon, dotted with specks of Bedouin fires as far as he could see.

"They will think you weak. Why give them any more reasons to doubt your authority?"

He shook the sandy soil out of his sandal. "I am weak because I don't want to command a herd of servant girls to do my bidding in bed? Then what does it mean to be strong?"

"Sebi deserves a virile man."

"Sebi is marrying a king, remember? I doubt she cares about bedroom abilities."

"Your sister will bear you many sons."

Seti walked on ahead. "I don't love her, and I don't want her to bear my children."

"Son, do not continue to speak of this!" She grabbed his elbow, her fingertips biting into his skin. "Amenmesse is waiting for you to take the wrong path. He will step in and claim the kingdom of Egypt."

"Let him."

"Your father would be ashamed of you!"

"His legacy is not one I want to be associated with."

"How dare you speak against him? His tomb is not even closed!"

"He hated me. I was not the ruthless son—I was the weakling. The embarrassment. I cannot rule Egypt as he did—by blood and terror. Amenmesse is the son who should have been firstborn."

"Please do not speak like this. You will anger the gods."

"They are already angry with me, Mother. And you only want me to be king so that you hold power, too. If Amenmesse rules, you have no power—unless he marries Sebi." He had never spoken his true feelings to his mother. *Has my father's death loosened my tongue?*

"I must protect you and your sister."

A pang of sorrow shot through his heart. She had borne him. His father's power had corrupted her and made her a self-centered and greedy woman.

"Mother, I shouldn't have spoken so harshly. I'm tired and much weighs on my mind. I need to go to the boat. All will be well tomorrow."

Indifference swept over him. Who was this woman, really? *Does she even care for me? Or is she so selfish she can't see beyond her own needs?* He kissed the top of her head.

"Very well. When I see you tomorrow, you will be king of Egypt. All these wild notions will be gone."

He nodded.

"I have dreamt of this day for a long time. Do not disappoint me. Tomorrow, my children will rule Egypt."

He watched her walk away then sighed. *Tomorrow.* When he was king, he could change the rules. Perhaps not the ones dictated by the gods, but the laws of the land could certainly be altered. The vastness of Egypt spread as far as one could travel in many days, in any direction he chose. *I am the most fortunate man alive. Why don't I feel like it?*

He made his way over the rocky path to the riverbank covered with low trees and scrub. The torch-lit launch lay in the distance. Drumming carried through the air, growing louder as he neared.

He stumbled and almost fell. "What?" Something brushed against his leg.

"Meow?"

"What are you doing out here?" He reached down and stroked the black feline that wrapped itself around his legs. "I'll bet you are looking for scraps.

Different colored eyes; how unusual."

The cat nuzzled him. He lifted it and rubbed his cheek against its head. "Why don't you come with me? I'd love a dinner partner." It purred. "A cat with a golden necklace? You must belong to someone special."

"Meow." It hopped out of his arms and trotted toward the boat launch.

"Let's go, then."

The animal led the way, occasionally stopping to wash or meow its impatience at his slower speed.

The cat stopped and sniffed the air then hissed, its fur bristling. It growled, low and long.

"What is it? Do you see an asp?" He crouched and patted its head.

With a sear of hot pain in his side and a whisper of *Amenmesse*, the world blackened.

Chapter Five

The cat licked Katharine's face.

"Fishy breath. Stop it, silly furball. I'll get up and feed you." She pushed the animal off her chest and sat up. A warm breeze blew across her. *I'm outside.*

"Meow?"

"What is going on?"

"Meow?"

"Not you! I'm talking to myself." Where the heck was she? No, hadn't been drinking. Probably not abducted, since she wasn't tied up or anything. Maybe sleepwalking? Yes, that had to be it. People did a lot of that when they were tired or stressed. She stood and stretched, her back a little stiff from lying on the ground. *How long have I been out here*?

The purring cat figure-eighted around her legs, and she picked it up. The moon hung low in the sky, full and round, but its light filtered across the landscape, barely illuminating any feature. Nothing looked familiar. Water trickled from nearby and she tried to determine where it originated. *How far did I walk*?

A low moan sounded behind her. She turned, her heart hammering in her throat. *Coyote*? The cat hopped out of her arms and walked in front of her a few steps then turned and meowed at her.

It disappeared into the underbrush about twenty feet away. She hurried to the spot then crouched down and peered into the darkness. The bush, heavy with the scent of musky flowers, parted in the middle.

A sandal. Two sandals. Two feet in two sandals. *A man!*

He moaned again and she backed away. Was he drunk? Hurt? *I have to call 911.* As she turned, she bumped into a tall woman.

"He'll die if we leave him here." she purred. "We have to help him."

"I-I was going to call 911."

"There are no telephones here. We have to save him. Do as I tell you and he has a chance. If not, they'll see his weakness and kill him."

Bile crept into her mouth as her adrenaline surged. *Kill?*

"Who's trying to kill him?"

The woman leaned closer. "I'll tell you everything once we get on the boat. Right now, both your lives are in danger. They already nearly killed him. You can save him."

Her eyes gleamed in the pale moonlight—one green and one blue. They seemed to be lit from within, and Katharine sensed power behind her words.

"I have to get home. I'll call 911."

"No time. He'll die."

"I got lost...I don't know where I am."

"Make a choice. Help me, and he lives. Otherwise, his life is over."

"Okay. How?"

"Let's get him out of the bushes. My name is Bast. I am his friend."

"I'm Katharine. Nice to meet you—even though the circumstances aren't the best."

"We need to hurry. Grab his ankles."

They tugged him, and she couldn't believe how heavy a man could be without having an ounce of obvious fat on him. Muscle weighed more and this man—hard and cut—was weighty. His shirtless chest, deep brown and smooth, bulged, and he wore some kind of loincloth or kilt. You didn't find a man this hot lying around just any day.

They edged him into the moonlight. His skin gleamed with perspiration, and his black hair brushed his shoulders. *It's probably not acceptable to fondle an injured man.* She shook her head. The man was injured, and someone was trying to kill him—and she stared at his chest. *I do need that one-night stand.*

On his side, just below his ribcage, blood coagulated on his skin in an oval patch. A puncture wound. Fortunately, not bleeding anymore. He winced, as she touched the sticky blood near the wound.

"It's deep," Katharine whispered.

"We need to get him out of here."

"Where are you taking me?" He struggled to sit.

"Be quiet if you wish to live," Bast said. "We're trying to save you."

His head bobbed once before he passed out. They dragged him a bit farther, and then pulled him to his feet.

"This way," Bast said. Each of them put an arm over her shoulders and they half dragged, half carried him down the path. "We need to get him on the boat. If we have to, we'll pretend he is drunk and we are his women for the night."

"What?" Katharine scrunched her nose.

Bast smiled. "It's half true."

She shook her head. Bast was about as wacky as Missy.

The drumming stopped as they approached the boat launch.

"Welcome, Seti." An old man stood on the dock, arms crossed and smiling.

"The vizier," Bast whispered.

Katharine gaped at the odd clothing and the torches—had she stepped onto the set of a reality television show?

Bast slumped Seti over onto Katharine and left her to support him on her own. She whispered to the vizier, and his eyes grew wide. He immediately waved the guards away and helped the women get Seti onto the boat.

"You must not let anyone stop you," he whispered. "I will see what I can do here."

"We'll sail straight to the house. Katharine is a doctor."

"I'm a vet—"

The vizier looked at her and scowled. "Wearing odd clothing. Are you sure you can save him?"

I'll try." She turned to the other woman. "Can we trust the oarsmen?"

Bast helped lower Seti to the deck. "Yes, they will protect him at all costs. But we have to leave before Amenmesse comes back."

"Hurry!" the vizier said. "The wind blows strongly tonight. Your sails will be full."

The boat rocked as the vizier moved from side to side. Katharine held on. How had this night gotten so crazy? *When did I agree to a boat ride?* "I need to go home." She moved to step ashore.

"I will help you get home soon," Bast said. "Please, help him. Madame Eve knew you would be the one to save him. She sent you."

"Excuse me?"

"She sent you to Seti. He is your chosen."

Katharine sat on the hewn bench. Her feet tingled. Every drop of blood was undoubtedly in her toes, and the swaying of the boat made her head spin. Her date was not only injured, but his attacker was on the loose.

"Eve?" Seti whispered. He moaned and slipped

into unconsciousness again.

Chapter Six

Seti fingered his side.

"Leave it alone. It'll get infected." The musical voice lilted with an unfamiliar accent. *Roman*? He tried to open his eyes, but they stung and filled with tears. His side throbbed.

"What happened?" he whispered.

"You were stabbed. We found you in the bushes by the river."

"My half-brother. He tried to kill me."

"What?"

"Amenmesse. He wants me dead."

"Why?"

A hand brushed his stomach and through the pain, flutters of desire rose through him. She pinched at his wound, and the desire rushed away. "Ouch! What are you doing?"

"Checking to see how deep it is. You need stitches, but I'm not equipped to handle that out here."

He groaned. *What nonsense is she talking?* "Where am I?" He squinted and saw the dome of the night sky above him, black. No moon in his field of vision, just darkness. *Maybe my eyes aren't really open.*

"We are on your boat, heading to your house. Bast is guiding the oarsmen."

"Bastet is here?" he raised his head, but the dizziness overtook him and he collapsed. *Oh, by the gods, it hurts.*

"Yes. Now lie still and let me clean your injury."

He listened to the rush of the water as they skimmed over it. *Will he attack the boat*? Maybe his half-brother presumed him dead. If only luck would hold out, he'd make it to the safety of the house.

"This'll sting," the woman said. "It's water."

A frigid coldness sliced through him, followed by a burning that bore into him like a hot stake. He shook, his teeth chattering. *By the gods....*

"I'm sorry. I know it hurts, but we have to get it clean."

She wrapped linen over his injury and around his back. Her hair trailed along his chest as she tied the bandage. Her touch was light as a butterfly flitting over his skin, and he kept his eyes closed, lest he spoil the magic. The phantom touches aroused him despite his pain, and he twisted to hide his state.

She covered him with a blanket and sat beside him.

"Thank you."

"You're welcome. I wish I'd had some antibiotic cream to put on your wound—it would feel a lot better."

Her hair brushed against his face, as the wind blew over the ship. He shivered.

"Bastet said Eve sent you," he said.

"About that...."

"She told me that Eve would send someone for me. Someone who would also need help." His head spun from speaking.

"Careful. Relax and try to rest. We can talk later." Her hand brushed his forehead.

He listened to the water lapping the sides of the boat for a few moments, feeling sleep on the edge of his consciousness. The night held mysteries—many more than the one's he'd expected. This woman, Eve, and Bastet. The gods mocked his indecision over taking his father's place by sending him puzzles he couldn't begin to unravel.

"What's your name?" he asked.

"Katharine."

"Lovely. I am Seti. I assume Bastet told you."

She pressed on his bandage. He groaned when the searing pain swept over him.

"You need to get to the hospital. I'm sure you need stitches."

"I don't know what you mean."

Her breath hitched.

"You're worried?" He raised his head.

"Lie down and rest." She lowered him to the thin mattress.

"I want to see you, but my vision is so cloudy."

"We're on a boat in the middle of a large river. I'm not going anywhere. I really need to be home working."

"Katharine?"

"Yeah?"

"Do you not want to be here with me?"

The pause lingered longer than it should have for a simple answer then he felt her hand on his chest. Warmth spread inside him, and he lay his hand over hers. *So loving. If only....*

"I'm glad I was here to help Bast get you to the boat. You could have died if no one found you."

"But you did. Eve sent Bastet to bring you to me. I feel it as surely as the Nile swells over the banks each season. You are meant to be here."

He listened to the night for a few minutes, waiting for her to speak more, perhaps tell him of her needs or wishes but she remained quiet. Was she looking at the stars? Or at him? His curiosity got the better of him and he opened his eyes, pushing back tears of pain. The moon wavered in the sky like a large pebble in the bottom of a pool, and he blinked to clear his vision. After a moment, the moon stilled and his head steadied. He turned to her, and his heart sped.

Divinity. Her hair, long and straight, pale as moonlight and as reflective as silver grain, waved around her face like a sea creature in the river breeze. Her lips were full and dark against her fair skin. Her nose, tiny and slightly upturned, looked like it had been molded from a flower petal. She watched the moon then turned to look at him. Joy streaked through him when she smiled. *By the gods, she must stay the night.*

"Can you help me sit?" He tried to push up with his hand, grasping the side of the boat for leverage.

"Whoa, hold on."

She put her arm around his shoulders. She smelled of sweet flowers and deep perfumes he didn't recognize, and he wanted to bury his face in her neck. His vision swirled as the pain spiked.

"Are you okay?"

He nodded, leaning against the side of the boat. The intoxicating scent of her lingered in his nose.

"Do you want some water?"

"Please." The odd garments she wore outlined her curves and legs. Perhaps the clothing was for travel. He followed the curve of her hip and leg down and back up again until she stood then he looked away.

The small rectangular sail furled and cracked in the wind. The vessel wasn't meant for more than a short trip down the river, but it sped along on the current and with the wind. The bare floor held a few woven mats for seating, and the long mattress he rested on would have been shielded by a canopy in daylight. Two oarsmen rowed at the far end and a shadowed figure stood with a long pole, steering.

"Bastet?"

"Hmm?" Katharine knelt on the mattress and

held a waterskin to his lips. He drank, the cool liquid filling his mouth and sliding down his throat. Close enough to smell, almost taste the scents that enveloped her, he leaned closer.

She moved to sit beside him.

"Is Bastet steering?"

"Yes."

"This night is unlike any I have had."

"Same here. Times ten." She pushed her hair away from her face. "How long does it take to reach your house? I need to call a cab so I can go home."

"The river runs quickly this season. But you don't need to leave on your cab tonight. Stay with me. We can go to town together in the morning." Surprise crossed her face and she shook her head.

"Oh, no. I have to go back tonight. I have work to do."

He reached for her hand and cupped it in his own. She trembled under his touch. "What work cannot wait until tomorrow? I owe you for saving me. And who would refuse a future king's request?"

Chapter Seven

*F*uture king? Maybe he hit his head when he fell. Or maybe she'd hit hers. The sleepwalking gig had gotten out of control. There wasn't a river near her house, nor any hot men walking around in loincloths. She'd been reading too many romance novels and now she was dreaming them. *Things are out of control.*

He squeezed her hand. "What's wrong? Do you not find me acceptable? Did Eve not bring us together so we could help each other?"

She gulped. That must be the explanation. The 1Night Stand date Missy had set up, combined with a long day at the clinic—she was sleeping hard and having the weirdest fantasies ever. She pinched herself.

"What are you doing?" He laughed, holding his bandaged side, then doubled over.

"Are you okay?"

He nodded. "Amenmesse will pay for this."

"Why would your own brother try to kill you?" *And why all the drama in my dream? I thought I just needed sex.*

"My half-brother." He blew out a long, slow breath. His dark lashes fluttered against his strong cheekbones, and she pushed his hair from his face.

"But why?"

"He wants the throne of Egypt. He thinks he should rule."

"Egypt?"

"Yes, I am firstborn son. By birthright, the

throne is mine. My father lies cold in his tomb and when the sun rises over the pyramids tomorrow, I will be crowned."

"You are telling me you are going to be a pharaoh?" *Crazier and crazier. I definitely have an imagination.*

"That is what some call it, yes. We call it king."

"But—"

Before she could finish her sentence, his lips pressed against hers and warmth spread to every part of her body. He pulled her closer and ran his tongue across her closed mouth. She whimpered.

"Katharine, you are meant to save me."

She backed away, creeping a few feet until her back hit the opposite side of the boat. *Outta control.* Yeah, she'd always had a thing for movies about sexy pharaohs, but this was ridiculous. "I want to wake up now."

"I want to wake up with you." His voice slurred. "I only wish I didn't have this injury. I could show you my power."

"You need to rest." *And I need to wake up.*

"I...am tired." He slumped, and she helped him lie back. For a moment, she leaned in to kiss him again then stopped.

"Katharine," Bastet called. "Come. I need to show you something."

Wobbly legged, she stood and made her way to the end of the boat where the other woman stood, steering.

"You don't believe," Bastet said. She swirled the long cane pole in the river current. The oarsmen, mute, rowed in silence.

"This is a dream."

"No, it isn't. Madame Eve brought you here. Believe. Seti needs you and right now; he needs someone to believe in."

Katharine watched Seti sleep. His hand lay over the bandage, and his chest rose and fell rhythmically. Even in the dark, his muscular chest and handsome face sent shivers through her.

"He thinks he is pharaoh. Of Egypt."

"And what do you think?"

"I think he must have had too much wine, or he hit his head after his brother stabbed him. He needs a hospital."

"Sit."

Katharine dropped onto the small seat beside Bast. The breeze lifted sounds from the banks and tossed them into the air. Frogs, insects, and other night creatures croaked and clicked. Fragrant blossoms lined the shore, filling the air with sweetness.

"It's so beautiful." The moonlight swam along the ripples on the water in wavy silver tendrils. Her shoulders dropped, and the tension rolled out of her back.

"It is." Bast moved the stick confidently, steering. "The Nile is life-giving, nurturing. The beginning of all things."

"The Nile."

"Yes. Madame Eve sent you to Egypt to find peace and possibly more. As difficult as it may be to believe, time does not flow in one direction."

"Meaning what? You don't expect me to believe I've traveled back in time?"

"That is what I'm telling you. Think of it this way. We are passengers on a river of time...."

"Yeah, I've heard that analogy before."

"Think of the mighty Nile as time itself. It flows south to north, which is somewhat unusual. But really, it isn't doing anything special—it is flowing along the path of least resistance. Downhill is the easiest direction—and holds fewer obstacles."

Bast stared out over the open water.

"Yes?"

"Well, as passengers on time's river, we steer toward the best way, too. Sometimes it means going in an unusual direction—like the Nile. You should trust that you are on your chosen path. It isn't the direction you expected—but it is the natural course."

Katharine yawned. Alice down the rabbit hole would have been an appropriate analogy, and things were becoming less weird by the moment. So what if she was in ancient Egypt? The time analogy made sense. She closed her eyes. *To dream within a dream.*

***

"Wake up." Bast said. "We're here. You're going to need to get him into the house without the guards realizing he's injured. Come on."

She rubbed her eyes. How long had she slept? The boat, grounded on a low bank, perched halfway out of the water. "Me? What about you?"

Bast was gone. Seti lay on the mattress, a small, dark shape resting on his chest. A brief pulse of bluish-green light flickered above him then all went dark. Voices called out from the bank, and the oarsmen disembarked. She needed to get him moving.

Chapter Eight

Seti winced, but when the expected pain didn't come, he sat up gingerly.

"Katharine, you are still here." The boat wobbled a little on the sandy bank, and he held his arms out to steady himself. "I feel so much better."

"You needed the rest."

"I am healed."

"Nonsense. You need to go to the hospital. First, we need to get you inside. Bast said not to let anyone see you are injured. Someone may tell Amenmesse."

"I feel fine. But thank you for staying with me." He put his arm around her and pulled her close, hiding the bandage. "We'll be safe once inside the walls."

"Let's go."

They stepped onto the muddy bank. As they reached the walkway, two guards cleared the edge of the embankment. He squinted at the bright torches.

"Lower the lights."

"A thousand pardons, my king," the taller guard said. "We've been expecting you."

"I'm here, and I wish to be left alone. Go."

The guard eyed Katharine. "She's dressed oddly."

"Her garments are not your concern."

The guard dipped his head. "Of course."

"Do not disturb us tonight. Let that be an order to everyone. No one enters the compound until sunrise, when I will emerge as Egypt's new king."

"As you wish. We'll give you the privacy you

require."

The gate snapped shut and Seti breathed in relief. "We made it," he whispered. "Let's go in. The house should be prepared to receive me."

He led her up a set of stone steps. Though the house was built for a king, it wasn't opulent, as the Nile flooding could wipe it away. Instead, it served as a resting retreat for the king and his companions. He'd been many times as a guest of his father, but never on his own.

The main room was large and open for talk or sleep. Pillows, stuffed mattresses, and woven mats spread from one end to the other. Large oil lamps flickered in every open space, lighting the room to almost daylight.

"Oh, the art is lovely." She ran her hands along the paintings of cats that sat on each side of the interior doors.

"Guardians. I am quite fond of cats."

She turned and her smile widened. "Me, too."

"I will have many in my father's, I mean, my palace." The urge to pull her close and lay her on the mattresses tore at his groin. His cock began to throb as he thought of taking her. When had a woman stirred him so, especially with a simple smile? *Never.*

"I've got quite a few, myself. And I take care of sick cats. I'm a veterinarian."

"What?"

"A cat doctor."

"No wonder you drew Bastet to you."

"Where did she go?" She gazed at the ceiling and the open-air skylights, the gentle curve of her neck open and exposed. The small black clothing she wore to hide her breasts didn't cover them completely, and the rounded tops lifted as she breathed. *Patience, by the gods....*

"The goddess comes and goes without sound."

"Okay...can we not talk any more about the craziness of this night? I feel like I am lost in wonderland."

Brushing her long hair over her shoulders, he shuddered. "I'm sure we have other things to discuss." He trailed his finger over her cheek, down her bare throat to her cleavage then back up her neck. Her skin, soft and unblemished, invited his touch. He licked his lips. "What would you like to talk about?" His voice, husky from the deepening draw to possess her, startled him. *I must have her.*

Before she could speak, he pressed his full lips against hers, his fingers entwined in her hair. She hugged him to her and met his kiss, gently. Her lips parted and he slid his tongue into her mouth and she responded with a thrust of her own. His head spun as he kissed her, and he pulled back, panting. *Got to slow down, or this will be a short night.*

"I want this to be perfect," he said, stroking her hair.

"I'm not sure a kiss could be more perfect."

His cock ached and grew rigid.

"Please don't stop."

He rubbed her face with his thumb, savoring the way she looked at him, innocent and lustful at the same time. Tomorrow was a world away—things would be back to work and politics. Tonight, he could be a man, not king.

Leading her to the largest mattress, he dimmed several of the lamps as they passed. Soft coverings of the finest silks in deep crimsons and blues draped over the bed, and pillows covered the floor around it.

"I need to take this off." He pulled the bandage loose and set it on the low table. *No pain.* He felt along his side. "I'm healed! The pain was gone, but this...?"

Her eyes widened. "How?"

"I think we know. The goddess would not allow my half-brother to take you from me. Come here."

She stood close, and he breathed in her scent, savoring her soft belly against his hardness. He'd never tire of her—his own exotic mixture of unknown flowers.

"You needed stitches."

"Shh. I'm healed. When will you start believing what is before your eyes?"

"Everything I believe has been turned upside down. I don't know what to believe."

"You feel me. You feel my passion for you. That is real."

She laid her head on his chest. His nipples hardened at her light touch. *How much longer can I wait?*

"What is that?"

On the table, beside the bandage he had discarded sat a small golden box with two jewels inlaid in the top. A blue stone and a green one. Bast. He opened the box. Inside were small foil packets. "Odd. I assume Bast left these, but what are they?"

Even in the torchlight, he saw her blush, as she ducked her head. "They are, uh, protection. For when we...uh. Do stuff."

He raised an eyebrow and then tore open one of the packets. Inside was a curious circular thing.

"Yeah, that goes there." She pointed.

The heat rose in his own face. "Ah," he said, dropping the item onto the table. "I see."

She giggled. He knelt in front of her and drew her into another kiss, entwining his strong tongue with her soft, wet one. When he could no longer bear it, he stopped.

"What is it?"

"Are you sure this is your course?"

"Yes. I'm sure."

"On the boat, you asked to go home. What has changed?"

She pushed him back and lay against him. "I've accepted my path. I want this, you, more than anything. I crave feeling your skin on mine as you move inside me."

Her light hair fanned out around her like sunshine. He smiled and ran his hand under the edge of her shirt, feeling the skin of her stomach quiver beneath his touch. Easing the shirt up and off, he watched as she slipped off the black undergarment. When she stood and dropped her lower garments, he gasped. He was used to seeing bare women, but her body called to him in ways he didn't understand other than a deep need to possess her.

"Your turn." She pointed to his clothing and quirked an eyebrow. She lay on the mattress, her pale skin glimmering.

He tripped over himself trying to disrobe so he could join her. She giggled as he steadied himself.

When he took her into his arms and bare skin met bare skin, his head dizzied and he closed his eyes to savor the sensation. His cock throbbed painfully and moved to find release. Her nipples hardened as he kissed her, and he nipped at her neck, drinking in her scent and kissing the soft flesh again and again.

He held her breasts in his hands and fingered the nipples, pinching them gently. She arched her back, her mouth half open. Need surged through his rigid cock, and he wanted to push into her warm wet mouth. His ache to possess her had grown beyond the bounds of return, and his restraint wavered. He longed to shove her down and take her.

He sucked, long and hard—teasing her nipples.

"Seti. Oh." She writhed under him.

He imagined her legs wrapped around him as he drove into her, again and again. His whole body trembled, and he reached between her legs and cupped her pussy. Wetness slid over his hand as he rubbed and slowly worked his finger inside her folds.

She flung her head back. When she moved against his finger, he edged in deeper thinking he would spill his seed all over her. *Keep control.* She held her eyes half open, but her hips bumped against him, and he moved his thumb to massage her most sensitive spot.

She tightened around his finger before she cried out. He buried his head in her hair and memorized the feeling of her bucking against him.

Chapter Nine

Katharine shook. Seti's dark complexion glowed warm in the lamp light, and he gazed at her with a hunger she'd only read about. No one had ever wanted her so much. She sensed his need and squeezed her legs together to hold on to her passion. He leaned over her, bending down to kiss her forehead. She reached under him, grabbing his hard cock then tugged it gently. He clambered to sit up on his knees, granting her unobstructed access.

His shaft pulsed, its velvety skin sliding through her hand. She cupped the head, touching the sticky moisture. When she shimmied up to be belly to belly with him, she grabbed his balls and squeezed. "You tease me," he moaned.

"I need this." *Oh, God, I need this.*

She continued to stroke and pull, and he met her rhythm. Her own desire pooled heavy between her legs, and she began working him close to her own center of pleasure. When his tip touched her pussy, she arched against him.

"I can't wait any longer to possess you," he said. "I want you now."

"Let me get a condom." She grabbed the golden box, snatched a packet, and ripped it open. He lay on his back on the mattress, his long heavy cock quivering as he tugged it.

"Hurry."

She straddled him and rolled the condom in place. When she started to move away, he grabbed her around the waist and sat her on his abdomen. Her wetness lay open on his stomach, and she ground against him.

"Now," he said.

He eased her onto him and she closed her eyes, feeling him fill her, inch by inch. He thrust deep, and she cried out.

Her breasts bobbed as she rode him. *So good.* His hands clasped her hips, guiding her up and down. He'd push the rhythm faster, and then slow down when she got close to release. Suddenly, he stopped.

"What's wrong? Don't stop."

"Look at the wall—look at us in the lamp light."

She looked at the erotic pose of their joining. He began moving again, and she watched the wall, mesmerized at the shadow bodies making love. Her back arched as he pushed deeper.

"Lean forward."

She bent toward him. He pushed into her, while the shadow man fucked the shadow woman on the wall. Tension coiled inside her from down low and began spiraling outward.

"Fuck me, Seti."

He quickened the pace, pounding into her.

She leaned against him, her climax exploding, as she opened to him.

His fingertips tightened on her hips, and he thrust into her harder, groaning and thrashing his head about until his own climax passed. He stilled.

She lay on his chest, her legs straddling him and his cock still inside her. The aftershocks of her orgasm rocked her, and she moved against him, trying to soak up the last bits of pleasure before they disappeared. *So good.*

She rolled off him and lay in his arms. *Is this merely a roll in the hay for him?* Nothing about the night felt normal. Seti was kind and had a way of looking right into her soul and calling her out—keeping her true to herself. He'd said stay the night. He wasn't ashamed. Why should she be?

"Katharine?" He stroked her hair.

"Yeah?"

"Thank you. I haven't bedded someone equal. Ever."

"Huh?"

"Usually sex is a very selfish dispensing of my own needs. Servants. They are always at the ready to provide release. But this...is more. I felt needed. I enjoyed pleasuring you as much as my own pleasure, if not more."

Okay, if this was ancient Egypt, then his words would make a lot more sense. Somewhere in them, there was a compliment—she was sure of it. "I enjoyed it, too. I won't forget our night together."

"I don't want it to end."

"We only have a night."

"Will you stay with me? Here? I know it would be different, perhaps difficult."

She sat up and pulled the silk blanket around her shoulders. "I have my clinic. And the cats. Besides, you must have a would-be queen."

He covered his face with his hands. "I am betrothed to my sister, Sebi, but I don't want to marry her. Amenmesse claims her, as well as Egypt. When the sun rises tomorrow, I will be in the middle of a very complicated political problem."

"You're going to marry your sister?"

"I don't love her. It is customary to marry within the family to strengthen bloodlines. My brother can have her—and all of Egypt. I don't want any of it."

"So don't marry her."

"It's complicated. My mother would kill me with her own hands if I didn't take Sebi as queen."

"If you are king, isn't it your choice?"

"Perhaps. I don't want to anger the gods."

Katharine sighed. This was messed up. "Well, we both have real lives, with real problems."

"Are you to marry someone you don't love?"

"No. I don't even have time to date. My clinic is operating in the red, and we owe a lot of money. I don't have enough time in the day to turn things around." Tears filled her eyes. "If I don't figure something out soon, I may lose the place—or have to stop helping so many stray and abandoned cats."

He stroked her hair. "You're a good person. Things will work out. You have to trust that you are on the right path."

"Why do people keep saying that to me?" *And why has the path been hidden for so long?*

"You must not be listening."

"I'm here, aren't I?"

"Yes. And I don't want to waste another moment thinking about tomorrow. Let's take some food out into the back garden and dine. The evening's activities have made me hungry."

What could it hurt? One night of paradise to compare all others to. "I hope the activities aren't over yet."

Chapter Ten

The garden inside the walled compound grew lush and green. They walked to the center, where the foliage parted and a mosaic floor lay shimmering in the moonlight. A small fountain bubbled nearby, and the night insects chirped and hummed. She only wore her black shirt and tiny undergarment, and he stared at her long legs when she bent to examine a bush.

"It's gorgeous. So many plants I've never seen." She ran her fingers along the edge of a large leaf. "I love the velvety texture of this one."

"My father created a garden to rival what he saw in his travels. He couldn't build hanging gardens here on the banks of the Nile, but he did build the irrigation system so that the plants would thrive." He set the basket of food on the mosaic. "The palace gardens are spectacular." Tracing the curve of her ass with his hand, he moaned. "Maybe you'll get to see them."

"Did he bring all these plants here?" She backed against him, and he wrapped his arms around her waist.

"In a way, yes. He had his envoys collect native plants wherever they went. Let me show you my favorite flower. Come."

"Okay."

He led her to the corner of the garden. "Look." He pointed to a viney plant that meandered up a tree and spilled out overhead, its underside dripping with violet blooms. The flowers hung low, swaying gently in the breeze.

"It smells divine. What is it?"

"Clematis. From the Orient. We have to replace them after every flood cycle. Only the strongest trees survive."

"Your father must have been a good man to care so much about living things. I'm sorry for your loss."

"No." He pulled down a branch of the flowering vine and plucked off the largest purple blossom. The center petals were streaked with fuchsia and tiny tendrils of bright yellow circled the middle of the flower. "Most are glad he is gone. I am."

"Why?"

"He was a selfish tyrant. He killed many for his own glorification."

"I'm sorry. You must have had a terrible childhood."

He tucked the lush blossom behind her ear. "It is what it is. Don't spoil the evening with talk of him. Let's eat."

She was fortunate not to have crossed paths with his father. Being from a different time had saved her from the king's wrath. *She'll go home soon. And I'll be left to rule. Alone.*

They ate in silence, side by side. The cool tiles of the mosaic provided both a table and seat for their small feast. The tiled artwork depicted an ocean scene, with fish and other sea creatures on a blue tiled background. *Another of my father's thefts.* He rubbed her knee, and she leaned against him. The warm breeze carried the honey almond scent of Clematis through the garden. Her hair brushed his back, and he shuddered.

"I've never seen so many stars; even in the bright moonlight they glitter. It's so clear here."

She gazed at the heavens, her long hair spilling across the warm tile. A streak of cold shot through his chest. *This night cannot end*! She was the one for him, he had no doubt. But if she remained in Egypt, her skin color would keep her from being accepted—even if he was king.

"I don't want you to leave."

"I don't want to leave, either, but I'm not sure we have a choice."

"There has to be a way." He pushed the basket and remaining food to the side. "This is too good to end."

"We still have time."

"Not as much as we need. The morning will be here soon."

"Yes, but we need to enjoy the here and now. Can we walk around the garden?" She stretched. Her body glowed in the moonlight, and his groin heated. Would there be time to bed her again?

They walked along the perimeter of the garden wall and he pointed out and named as many plants as he could remember. She stopped and kissed him.

"I want you," she said. "Here. Now."

His cock hardened. No one had ever spoken to him like that. No one had dared.

She pushed him against the wall and knelt. As she undid his garment, she looked up at him. "My turn."

He wasn't sure what she meant until her wet mouth closed over him and his knees buckled. Her tongue ran over the underside of his cock and she planted kisses along his length. When she squeezed his balls and took him into her mouth, he moaned. *Bliss.*

She stroked and sucked until his entire body buzzed and he verged on exploding. *By the gods, how much more?*

"Yes." He cradled her head in his hands and pulled her forward again and again. As the pressure built, he leaned his head back, waiting on release. She moved in a hard rhythm, and his balls drew up just before he spilled warmth into her mouth. "Oh." He collapsed, the wall steadying him.

"Feel good?"

"I didn't realize such pleasure was possible." He pulled her to him, his heart thudding against her soft breasts.

"If we only had time, I'd show you more."

Chapter Eleven

Katharine watched Seti sleep, his dark lashes fluttering as he dreamed. How was this night possible? Did it matter? They had talked for hours and made love again out in the garden before coming inside to rest. The night had been beyond her wildest fantasies. Seti knew how to pleasure her and reach her heart at the same time. Even though she'd met him a few hours before, he fit right into her soul. *He completes me.*

The open-air skylight above them showed night was almost over. It wasn't quite dawn, but close enough the sky was beginning to lighten. Whatever was going on, Bast was the key.

Katharine ran her hand along the trail of dark hair between Seti's navel and his garment. The silky hair was thin, but still showed the path to nirvana. She reached farther down and cupped his cock. It hardened a little, and she squeezed.

He pushed into her hand. "I worried I'd wake up and you'd be gone."

"I'm not leaving until I have to."

"Then let's make the most of our time."

"Again? Really?"

"Do you doubt a king's passion?" His dark eyes sparkled with mischief. "Do I need to order you to spread yourself for me?"

Wetness soaked her panties. "Order me."

She leaned in for a kiss. As her lips met his, there was a rap at the door.

Seti sat up. "What do you want?"

The knocking became banging. "Let us in. You cannot escape this time, brother."

"Amenmesse! He'll kill us both. Hide in the garden, quick!"

"I'm not leaving you. Ever." She clutched his hand. *Is this the end?*

"Let us in, Seti. You don't deserve to be king. It should have been my birthright."

"You can have it."

Amenmesse laughed and the deepness shook Katharine. The man was bad.

"I have to kill you. Otherwise, I can't take the throne of Egypt or bed Sebi." He banged on the door again. "Open up. Face me like a man."

"I'm scared," she whispered. Her hands trembled and he took them in his own, larger hands and squeezed them.

"Don't worry. My guards are out there."

"Unless his men killed them."

"Break the door down," Amenmesse shouted.

She shivered. "They're coming in. We can't stop them."

"Meow?"

"Bastet!" He pointed to the skylight. Katharine saw the cat peering over the edge of the opening.

The animal leapt into the room and morphed into a woman.

"Oh, my goddess!"

"Bast! How? You were the cat that came to my clinic?" Katharine's head spun. "Help us! Amenmesse will kill us."

The thudding grew louder and the door creaked.

"It's time to choose your path," Bast said. "Will you rule this land?"

"My path is with Katharine."

She clung to him.

"Do you want to be with me?" Seti held her at arm's length. She nodded. Terror struck her speechless as the door began to give way. "Bastet, I don't want to be king. Please tell me you understand."

The woman smiled. "You two are blessed. The fates have united you on a single path. Take this." She handed Seti her necklace. The green stone glowed. "Now hold her."

The door gave way and men rushed into the room, daggers drawn. Katharine closed her eyes, as the world gave way beneath her feet.

"Look."

She peered between her fingers. Her desk, piled with paperwork, sat in front of her. "Amenmesse?"

"Gone. And we still have each other. I don't know where we are, but we are together."

"It's my office. I'm home."

Nothing had changed. *How long have I been gone?* Darkness lay outside the window, and her blanket was piled on the floor.

"Look what I brought." Seti held up the golden box of condoms.

She laughed. "Fast thinking. But we do have plenty of those here."

"I wanted to be ready. And we can sell the box. Surely it is worth enough to help you."

His thoughtfulness touched her heart. Never mind the issues they had yet to face—he was here and they were together. Perhaps they could return to Egypt one day and straighten things out.

He held out the necklace. She fingered the green pendant and wondered when Bast would return. She'd never look at cats the same way again.

Pulling her close, Seti stroked her hair. "We walk the path together now, Katharine."

About Kerry Adrienne

Kerry loves history and spends large amounts of time wondering about people who lived and walked on Earth in the past.

In addition to writing, she's a college instructor, costumer, painter, and editor. Her new love is her Mini Cooper Convertible, Sheldon, and they have already gone on many adventures. Her family currently has seven cats (two Bengals and five rescues), a panther chameleon, a lionhead miniature bunny, and a leopard gecko.

You can visit Kerry at:
http://kerryadrienne.com/

www.ingramcontent.com/pod-product-compliance
Lightning Source LLC
Chambersburg PA
CBHW061242170626
46809CB00007B/2793